food &
fuel
$1.49 a
PINT
Special
99¢
6/59¢
50¢
all
SODA
we
got
SLURPS
1.49
MILK
ice cream
bars 39¢
OPEN
Phone
Pitch
in
Flips

THE LOUD HOUSE

#16 "LOUD AND CLEAR"

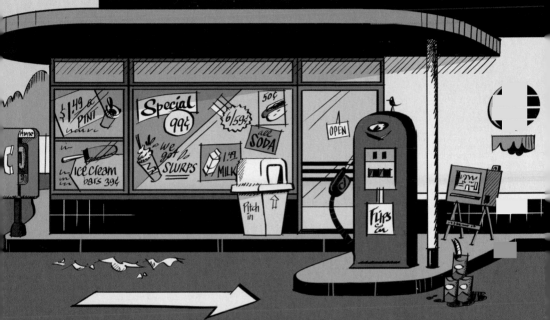

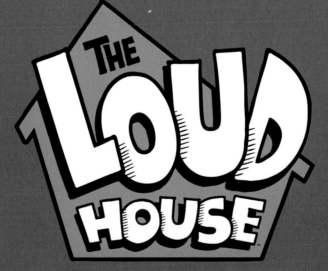

PAPERCUTZ
New York

MORE GREAT GRAPHIC NOVEL SERIES AVAILABLE FROM
PAPERCUTZ™

THE SMURFS TALES

BRINA THE CAT

CAT & CAT

THE SISTERS

ATTACK OF THE STUFF

LOLA'S SUPER CLUB

SCHOOL FOR EXTRATERRESTRIAL GIRLS

GERONIMO STILTON REPORTER

THE MYTHICS

GUMBY

MELOWY

BLUEBEARD

GILLBERT

ASTERIX

FUZZY BASEBALL

THE CASAGRANDES

THE LOUD HOUSE

ASTRO MOUSE AND LIGHT BULB

GEEKY F@B 5

THE ONLY LIVING GIRL

papercutz.com
Also available where ebooks are sold.

THE LOUD HOUSE

#16 "LOUD AND CLEAR"

nickelodeon THE LOUD HOUSE

#16 "LOUD AND CLEAR"

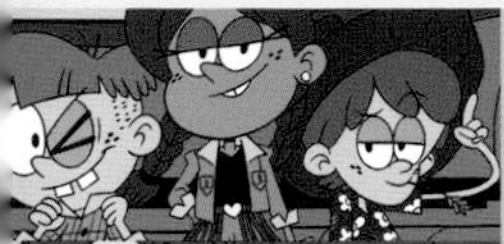

"TAKEOUT FAUX PAS"
Mariah Wilson — Writer
Jennifer Hernandez — Artist, Colorist
Wilson Ramos Jr. — Letterer

"SKATE-OFF OF GLORY"
Kara and Amanda Fein — Writers
Lex Hobson — Artist, Colorist
Wilson Ramos Jr. — Letterer

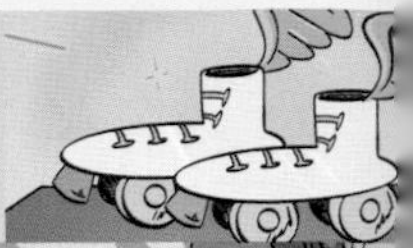

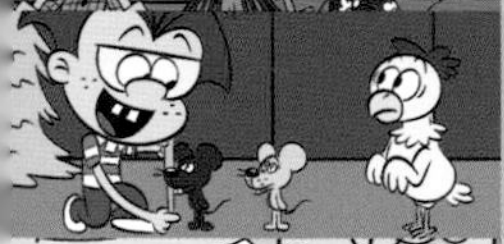

"BARNYARD BLUES"
Kara Fein — Writer
D.K. Terrell — Artist, Colorist
Wilson Ramos Jr. — Letterer

"STORY GAME BLAME"
Amanda Fein — Writer
Lex Hobson — Artist, Colorist
Wilson Ramos Jr. — Letterer

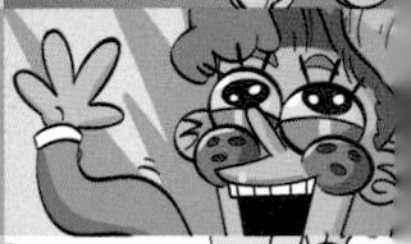

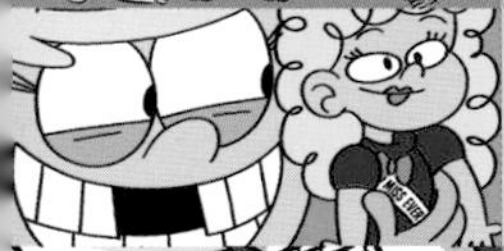

"WHATTA DOLL"
Amanda Fein — Writer
Amanda Lioi — Artist, Colorist
Wilson Ramos Jr. — Letterer

"UNIFORM UPHEAVAL"
Kiernan Sjursen-Lien — Writer
Erin Hyde — Artist, Colorist
Wilson Ramos Jr. — Letterer

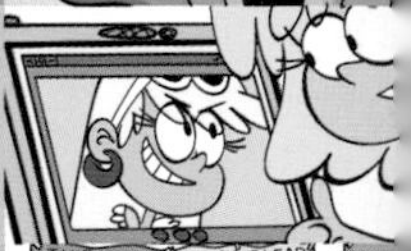

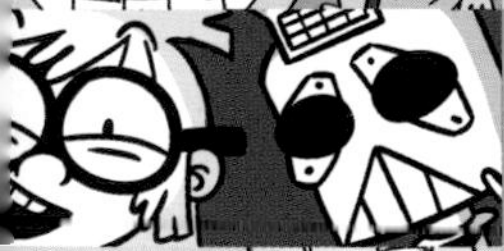

"IT'S ALIVE!"
Erik Steinman — Writer
Amanda Tran — Artist, Colorist
Wilson Ramos Jr. — Letterer

"FLYER FACE-OFF"
Kiernan Sjursen-Lien — Writer
Amanda Lioi — Artist, Colorist
Wilson Ramos Jr. — Letterer

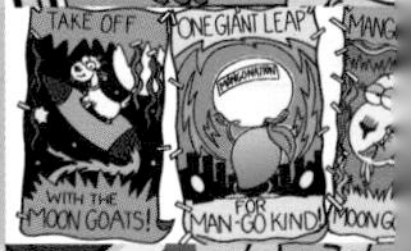
TAKE OFF
WITH THE MOON GOATS!
ONE GIANT LEAP
FOR MAN-GO KIND!

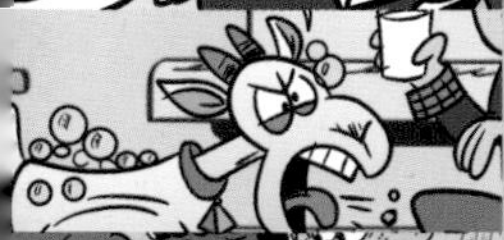

"FOR-GOAT-EN RECIPE"
Mariah Wilson — Writer
Zazo Aguiar — Artist, Colorist
Wilson Ramos Jr. — Letterer

"A BIG, BIG WORLD"
Kiernan Sjursen-Lien — Writer, Artist
Erin Rodriguez — Colorist
Wilson Ramos Jr. — Letterer

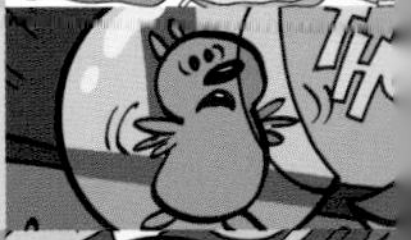

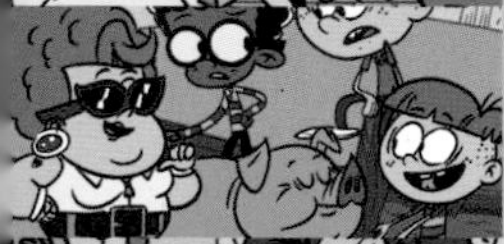

"MEE MAWLICE"
Derek Fridolfs — Writer
Zazo Aguiar — Artist, Colorist
Wilson Ramos Jr. — Letterer

"LOUD OF THE THRONES"
Kiernan Sjursen-Lien — Writer, Artist
Erin Rodriguez — Colorist
Wilson Ramos Jr. — Letterer

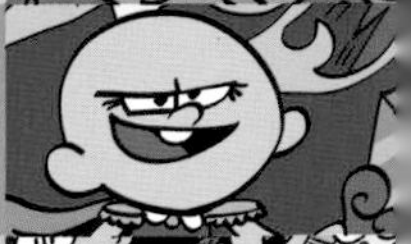

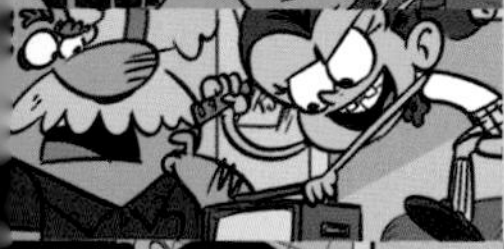

"FLIP'S FLOPS"
Derek Fridolfs — Writer
Zazo Aguiar — Artist, Colorist
Wilson Ramos Jr. — Letterer

"HIDE-AND-CHIC"
Erik Steinman — Writer
Amanda Tran — Artist, Colorist
Wilson Ramos Jr. — Letterer

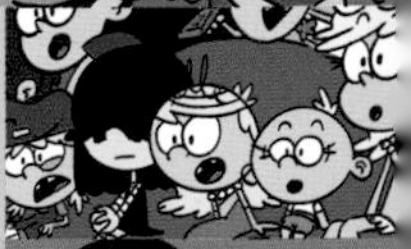

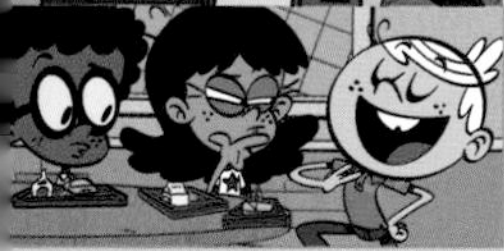

"STRIPES"
Jair Holguin — Writer
Lex Hobson — Artist, Colorist
Wilson Ramos Jr. — Letterer

"MEOW OR NEVER"
Paloma Uribe — Writer
Amanda Tran — Artist, Colorist
Wilson Ramos Jr. — Letterer

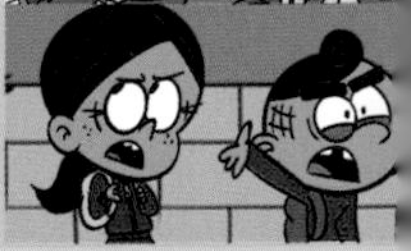

MAX ALLEY — Cover Artist
PETER BERTUCCI — Cover Colorist
JORDAN ROSATO — Endpapers
JAYJAY JACKSON — Design
KRISTEN G. SMITH, DANA CLUVERIUS, MOLLIE FREILICH, NEIL WADE, MIGUEL PUGA, LALO ALCARAZ, JOAN HILTY,
KRISTEN YU-UM, EMILIE CRUZ, AND ARTHUR "DJ" DESIN— SPECIAL THANKS
KARLO ANTUNES — EDITOR
STEPHANIE BROOKS — ASSISTANT MANAGING EDITOR
JEFF WHITMAN — COMICS EDITOR/NICKELODEON
MICOL HIATT — COMICS DESIGNER/NICKELODEON
JIM SALICRUP
Editor-in-Chief

ISBN: 978-1-5458-0889-4 paperback edition
ISBN: 978-1-5458-0888-7 hardcover edition

Papercutz books may be purchased for business or promotional use. For information on bulk purchases please contact Macmillan Corporate and Premium Sales Department at (800) 221-7945 x5442.

Printed and bound in China
August 2022

Distributed by Macmillan
First Printing

MEET THE LOUD FAMILY

and friends!

LINCOLN LOUD
THE MIDDLE CHILD

At 12 years old, Lincoln is the middle child, with five older sisters and five younger sisters. He has learned that surviving the Loud household means staying a step ahead. As the "man with a plan," he's always coming up with a way to get what he wants or deal with a problem, even if things inevitably go wrong. But don't worry, Lincoln's got a backup plan for that, too. He loves comic books, video games, magic, fantasy and science fiction stories – all of which you might find him enjoying in his underwear. His favorite characters include secret agent David Steele (think James Bond), superhero Ace Savvy (think Superman with a knack for playing-card puns) and video game protagonist Muscle Fish. He and his best friend Clyde make up the dynamic duo, Clincoln McCloud! They, along with his best friends (collectively known as "the Action News Team" because of the reporting they do for the school news program), always stick together – it's the best way to survive middle school.

LORI LOUD
THE OLDEST

At 17, Lori's the first-born child of the Loud clan, and therefore sees herself as the boss of all her siblings. She feels she's paved the way for them and deserves extra respect. Her signature traits are rolling her eyes, texting her boyfriend Bobby (AKA "Boo-Boo Bear"), and literally saying "literally" all the time. Because she's the oldest and most experienced sibling, Lori can be a great ally, so it pays to stay on her good side, especially since she can drive.

Lori has begun attending Fairway University, a prestigious golf college, and is one of the youngest players to make the school's golf team. Even though she's moved away from home, she's always in touch with her siblings. Even at college, Lori is always part of the Loud family shenanigans.

LENI LOUD
THE FASHIONISTA

Sixteen-year-old Leni spends most of her time designing outfits, accessorizing, and shopping at the mall – which makes her the perfect sales employee at Reininger's department store. Her people-pleasing nature, natural leadership abilities, and fashion instincts keep customers coming back! Leni is supported by her best friends and co-workers, Miguel and Fiona (and sometimes Tanya the mannequin). And now she has the added support of her new boyfriend, Gavin, who works in the mall food court.

Back at the house, she always falls for Luan's pranks, and sometimes walks into walls when she's talking (she's not great at doing two things at once). But what Leni lacks in smarts, she makes up for in heart. She's the sweetest Loud around!

LUNA LOUD
THE ROCK STAR

Luna, 15, is loud, boisterous and freewheeling, and her energy is always cranked to 11. On the off-chance she doesn't have her guitar with her, everything can and will be turned into a musical instrument. You can always count on Luna to help out, and she'll do most anything you ask, as long as you're okay with her supplying a rocking musical accompaniment.

When she's not jamming, Luna is most likely hanging out with her girlfriend, Sam, or playing with their band, The Moon Goats. The two might even be found babysitting the McBride's cats – it turns out Sam's a natural cat whisperer!

MR COCONUTS

Luan Loud's wisecracking dummy.

LUAN LOUD
THE JOKESTER

Luan, 14, is a standup comedienne who provides a nonstop barrage of silly puns. She's big on prop comedy – squirting flowers and whoopee cushions – so you have to be on your toes whenever she's around. She loves to pull pranks – April Fool's Day is her favorite day (and the rest of the Louds' least favorite). Luan is also a really good ventriloquist – she is often found doing bits with her dummy, Mr. Coconuts (but don't let him hear you calling him a "dummy"). At school, Luan and her boyfriend, Benny, are usually writing and performing in the high school's theatrical productions – under the somewhat melodramatic supervision of their drama teacher, Mrs. Bernardo. Luan has also reached new heights while playing Dairyland character Heidi Heifer during the theme park's season.

LYNN LOUD
THE ATHLETE

Lynn, 13, is athletic, full of energy, and always looking for a challenge or competition. She can turn anything into a sport. Putting away eggs? Jump shot! Score! Cleaning up the eggs? Slap shot! Score! Despite her competitive nature, Lynn always tries to have a good time with her family... and her teammates and best friends Paula and Margo. At school, she takes her duties as hall monitor seriously and doesn't tolerate any slackers... but she also shows a lot of heart when looking after Lincoln in his first year at middle school. One super fun fact about Lynn: her name is really Lynn Jr. (L.J.), because she's named after Dad!

LUCY LOUD
THE EMO

Eight-year-old Lucy can always be counted on to give the morbid point of view in any given situation. She is obsessed with all things spooky and dark – funerals, vampires, séances... you get the idea. Lucy has a way of mysteriously appearing out of nowhere, and try as they might, her siblings never get used to this. She loves the character of Edwin from the TV show "Vampires of Melancholia," and has a homemade bust of him hidden in her closet.
Lucy spends most of her time with her friends in the Morticians Club, of which she's a co-president. Together, the club speaks to spirits, attends casket conventions, and rides around in a hearse (well, technically it's just a station wagon painted black). Their motto is "Keep Calm and Embalm."

LOLA LOUD
THE BEAUTY QUEEN)

Lola, 7, is a pageant powerhouse whose interests include glitter, photo shoots, and her own beautiful, beautiful face. But don't let her cute, gap-toothed smile fool you; underneath all the sugar and spice lurks a Machiavellian mastermind. Whatever Lola wants, Lola gets – or else. She's the eyes and ears of the household and never resists an opportunity to tattle on troublemakers. But if you stay on Lola's good side, you've got yourself a fierce ally – and a credit line to the first national bank of Lola. She might even let you drive her around in her pink jeep while she practices her pageant wave.

LANA LOUD
THE TOMBOY

Lana is the rough-and-tumble sparkplug counterpart to her twin sister, Lola. She's all about animals, mud pies, and muffler repairs. She's the resident Ms. Fix-it and animal whisperer, and is always ready to lend a hand – the dirtier the job, the better. Need your toilet unclogged? Snake trained? Back-zit popped? Lana's your gal. All she asks in return is a handful of kibble (she often sneaks it from the dog bowl anyway) or anything you can fish out of a nearby garbage can. She's proud of who she is, and her big heart definitely overpowers her pungent dumpster smell. Needless to say, while the twins love each other deep down, they've been known to get into some pretty epic brawls, mud and sequins flying. But when they join forces (like the time they pretended to be each other for their own personal gain), the rest of the Louds had better look out.

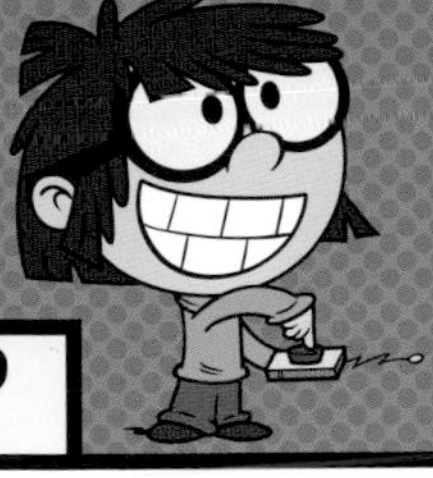

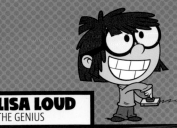

LISA LOUD
THE GENIUS

Lisa is smarter than the rest of her siblings combined, which would still be big news even if she wasn't only four years old. Lisa spends most of her time working in her bedroom lab (the family has gotten used to the explosions), and says her research leaves little time for frivolous pursuits like "playing" or "human interaction." Despite this, she can still find time to unwind with a little bit of West coast rap. She has a collection of robot companions that she's created over the years, but these days relies mostly on Todd, her newest (and sassiest) mechanical friend. Together they've traveled back in time, launched themselves into outer space, and enjoyed many hours watching Todd's favorite TV show, "Robot Dance Party." At school (where Lisa is smarter than her teacher), she is learning to enjoy social interaction with her friend Darcy, but will forego nap time to work on all the top secret projects she's got going on with the Norwegian government.

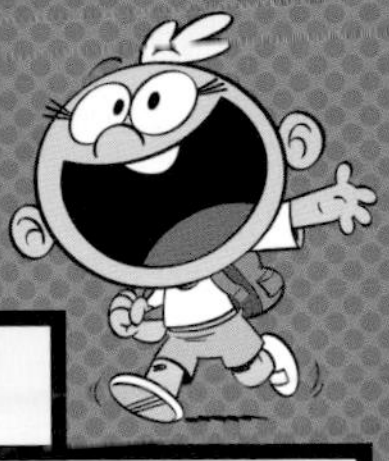

LILY LOUD
THE BABY

Lily's the baby of the family, but she's growing up fast. She's a toddler now and can speak full sentences– well, sometimes. As an infant she was already mischievous, but now she's upped her game. Her most important goal – other than tricking the family into taking her for ice cream – is to impress the other pre-school kids at show and tell. No matter what, though, she still brings a smile to everyone's faces, and the family loves her unconditionally.

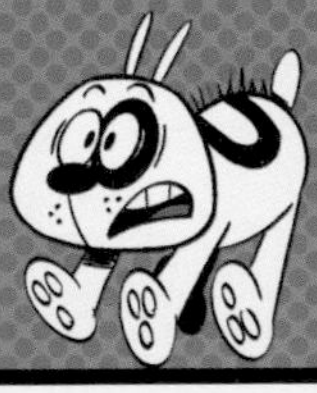

CHARLES

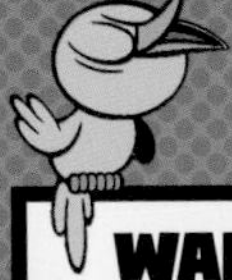

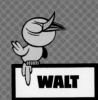

WALT

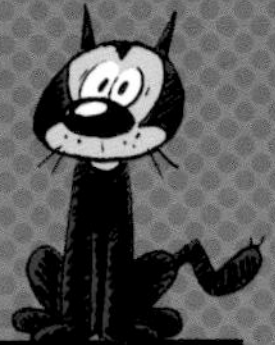

CLIFF

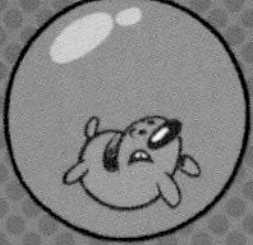

GEO

RITA LOUD

Mother to the eleven Loud kids, Mom Rita wears many different hats. She's a chauffeur, homework-checker and barf- cleaner-upper all rolled into one. Mom is organized and keeps the family running like a well-oiled machine. She's always there for her kids and ready to jump into action during a crisis, whether it's a fight between the twins or finding Leni's missing shoe. When she's not chasing the kids, she's a columnist for the Royal Woods Gazette. As a skilled writer, she's able to connect with her readers as a mom simply trying to do her best. She also loves taking on house projects and is very handy with tools (guess that's where Lana gets it from). Between writing her novel, working on her column, and being a mom, her days are always hectic - but she wouldn't have it any other way.

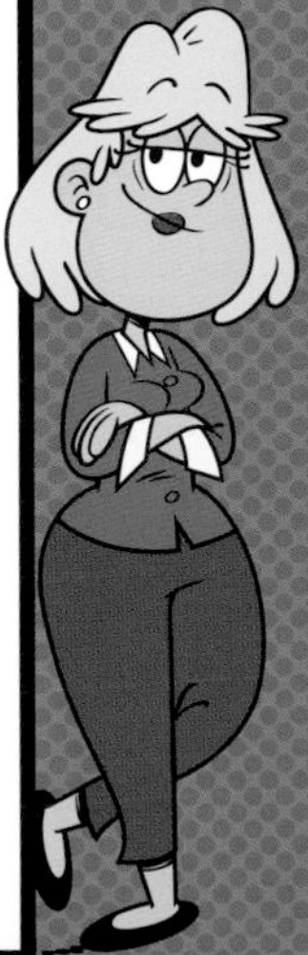

LYNN LOUD SR.

Dad (Lynn Loud Sr.) is a fun-loving, upbeat chef and owner of Lynn's Table – a family style restaurant that specializes in serving delicious but outrageously named meals like Lynn-sagna and Lynn-ger chicken. A sentimental kid-at-heart, he's not above taking part in the kids' zany schemes but is more well known for the emotions he wears on his sleeves: his sobbing – both for joy and sadness – is legendary. In addition to cooking, Dad loves his van (affectionately named Vanzilla), British culture, and making puns with any of the kids not already rolling their eyes. Most of all, Dad loves rocking out with his best friend and head waiter, Kotaro. They're part of a cowbell-focused band with some other dads in Royal Woods; hence their band name: The Doo-Dads.

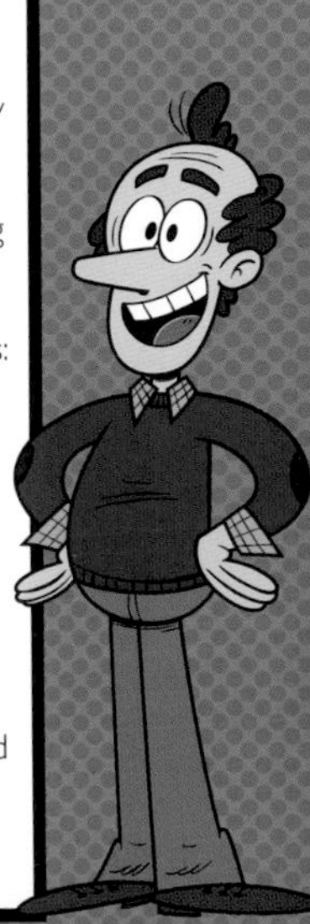

LINDSAY SWEETWATER

CLYDE McBRIDE
THE BEST FRIEND

Clyde is Lincoln's best friend in the whole world… so it probably goes without saying that he's also Lincoln's partner in crime. Clyde is always willing to go along with Lincoln's crazy schemes, even if he sees the flaws in them up-front or if they sometimes give him anxiety tummy aches. Lincoln and Clyde are two peas in a pod and share pretty much all of the same tastes in movies, comics, TV shows, toys—you name it. Clyde knows exactly who he is and is not afraid to show it! As an only child, Clyde envies Lincoln—how cool would it be to always have siblings around to talk to? But since Clyde spends so much time at the Loud house, he's almost an honorary sibling anyway. Clyde is a little neurotic, but that's probably because he's the son of helicopter dads, Howard and Harold. They are VERY over-protective and VERY involved in his life. Clyde isn't spoiled, he's just extremely well-cared for. But he's slowly learning to stand on his own two feet and his Dads are starting to see how well he can take care of himself.

ZACH GURDLE

Lincoln's pal Zach is a self-admitted nerd who's obsessed with aliens and conspiracy theories. (He's just following in the footsteps of his alien hunting parents.) Zach lives between a freeway and a circus, so the chaos of the Loud House doesn't faze him. To Zach, everything is a mystery to be solved or coverup to be exposed. His best friend in the gang is Rusty, with whom he occasionally butts heads. But deep down, it's all love.

RUSTY SPOKES

Lincoln's friend Rusty is a self-proclaimed ladies' man who's always the first to dish out girl advice— even though he's never been on an actual date. No one has more confidence than Rusty, even if that confidence is often completely misguided. Rusty's a looker – at least in his own eyes – and is always working hard to protect his face (what he calls his "moneymaker"). Rusty is always sharing advice from his experienced but equally delusional cousin, Derek. No matter what the situation, it seems like Derek's been there before and lived to tell about it. Rusty's dad, Rodney, owns a clothing store called "Duds for Dudes," so he can always hook the gang up with some dapper duds—just as long as no one gets anything dirty.

LIAM HUNNICUTT

Lincoln's friend Liam is an enthusiastic, sweet-natured farm boy full of down-home wisdom. He loves hanging out with his Mee Maw, wrestling his prize pig Virginia, and sharing his farm-to-table produce with the rest of the gang. No matter the situation, Liam faces it with optimism.

STELLA ZHAU

Lincoln's pal Stella is a tech genius, always building new devices – usually from part she's salvaged from old devices. She loves to take things apart just to see how they work. Her smarts help keep the gang focused and on track, especially when they're chasing a news story. Stella will happily take charge of a situation – she's helped solve many a school mystery, and even improved the gang's shield formation defense in dodgeball.

SAM SHARP

Sam is Luna's girlfriend and a member of the Moon Goats. She's sweet and kind, and is able to keep her feet on the ground even as she and Luna dream of a famous future. She helps keep Luna grounded, too, always turning a negative (the fact they may not have much in common at first) into a positive (it gives them so many new things to do together).

MAZZY

Mazzy is Luna's classmate at Royal Woods High School, and the drummer in her band, The Moon Goats. Mazzy has a cool rocker fashion vibe, a witty, dry sense of humor, and a pet tarantula.

SULLY

Sully is also Luna's classmate and a member of The Moon Goats. He's known for his chill, lowkey attitude – nothing rattles him. Sometimes, though, it takes him a moment or two to catch on to what's happening around him.

FLIP

Flip is the owner of Flip's Food and Fuel, the local convenience store. Flip has questionable business practices; he's been known to sell expired milk and soak his feet in the nacho cheese! Flip's a tough businessman; there's nothing he wouldn't do to save a buck. Flip also goes by several aliases, all of whom also operate odd businesses in Royal Woods: Tony, of Tony's Tows N Toes, Tucker of Tucker's Tix N Tux, and Pat of Pat's Prawn N' Pawn's, etc. Flip's got a huge soft spot for the high school gal that got away, turkey mogul Tammy Gobblesworth, and is tickled to have rekindled a relationship with her now.

MEE MAW

Mee-Maw is Liam's no nonsense grandmother. She's in charge of running the family farm, so she's all business; she doesn't like folks wasting her precious time. But despite her serious attitude out in the fields, she's all heart when it comes to her favorite grandson (and her favorite pig, Virginia). Like Liam, she often spouts serious down-home wisdom.

TODD BOT

While Todd is just one of the many robots Lisa's built, he's definitely her favorite (ssshh, don't tell the others!). He's outspoken and opinionated, and sometimes a little too sassy for Lisa (which is why she installed a button to dial down the sassiness). Still, she relies on him for everything, from coordinating scientific presentations worldwide, to building rockets and time travel devices, to providing a funky beat she can rap to. Todd is a loyal companion to Lisa - except, you know, when someone accidentally flips his "villain" switch, and then he just wants to destroy Royal Woods (but this rarely happens so it's all good).

BENNY STEIN

Benny is Luan's classmate, co-star and, most importantly, boyfriend. He's shy and quirky, but also sweet and earnest. He's not a zany comedian like Luan, but he sure enjoys her sense of humor and appreciates her wicked skills when it comes to prop comedy. Whenever he's too shy to speak for himself, he speaks through his ventriloquist's dummy, Mrs. Appleblossom—who has a Mrs. Doubtfire-esque British accent.

SHANNON

Shannon's a classmate of Luan's and part of the drama department at Royal Woods High School. She's very focused on her acting career and is super excited for any chance she gets to stand in the spotlight. Because of that, she sometimes ruffles feathers by either working her way to center stage or going off script to make the character more her own.

SPENCER

Spencer is another classmate of Luan's and part of the Royal Woods High School drama department. Unlike Shannon, however, he's super happy with any role he gets, be it "announcer guy" or "clown judge number three." The adage "there are no small parts" was definitely created with Spencer in mind.

MARGO

Margo is Lynn's best friend and teammate, and a fellow sports fan. She shares Lynn's passion for greasy food and never turns down a trip to the Burpin' Burger. Margo is enthusiastic and energetic, but also tends to be easy-going and humble. She's a great friend to Lynn and always supportive of her.

PAULA

Paula is a classmate, teammate, and friend of Lynn's. She's kind of an amazing athlete, considering she plays soccer, basketball, and even football with a broken leg – poor Paula's been using a crutch since we met her! She's been known to needle Lynn and their friend Margo, constantly pointing out moments where one of the girls should feel awkward or uncomfortable.

MRS. BERNARDO

Kate Bernardo is Luan and Benny's drama teacher at Royal Woods Middle School. And she's well-suited for the job, since no one is more dramatic than her. Every moment of her life is performed to the hilt, with abundant (and exhausting) flair and flourishes. Mrs. B is always performing a new one-woman show, covering scintillating topics like the time her waitress application at Dad's restaurant was rejected, and touting her extensive acting resume, including her prized role as "nervous customer number one" in a TV commercial that only aired once on a late night cable show.

"TAKEOUT FAUX PAS"

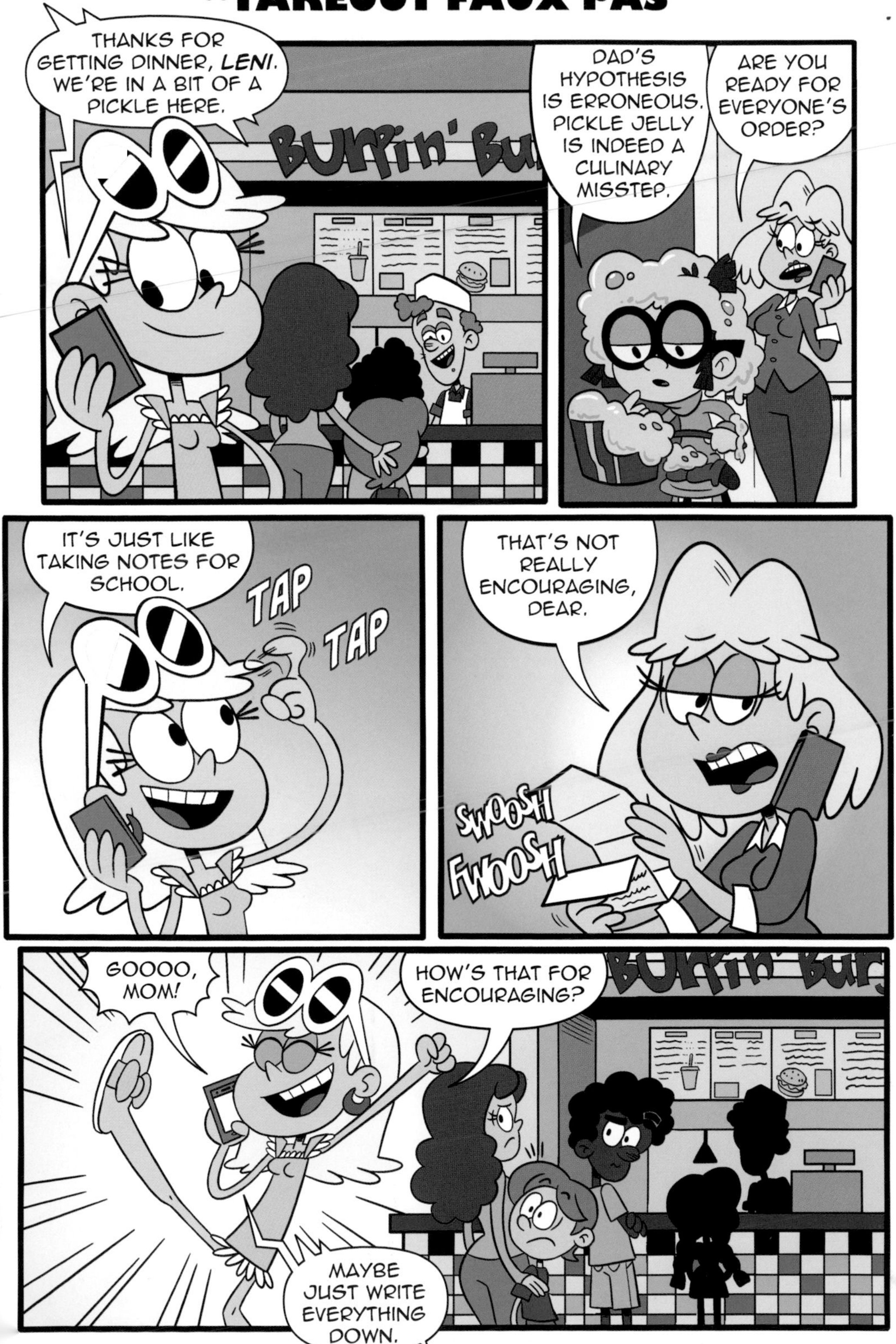

THANKS FOR GETTING DINNER, *LENI*. WE'RE IN A BIT OF A PICKLE HERE.
BURPIN' BU
DAD'S HYPOTHESIS IS ERRONEOUS. PICKLE JELLY IS INDEED A CULINARY MISSTEP.
ARE YOU READY FOR EVERYONE'S ORDER?
IT'S JUST LIKE TAKING NOTES FOR SCHOOL.
TAP
TAP
THAT'S NOT REALLY ENCOURAGING, DEAR.
SWOOSH
FWOOSH
GOOOO, MOM!
HOW'S THAT FOR ENCOURAGING?
BURPIN' BUR
MAYBE JUST WRITE EVERYTHING DOWN.

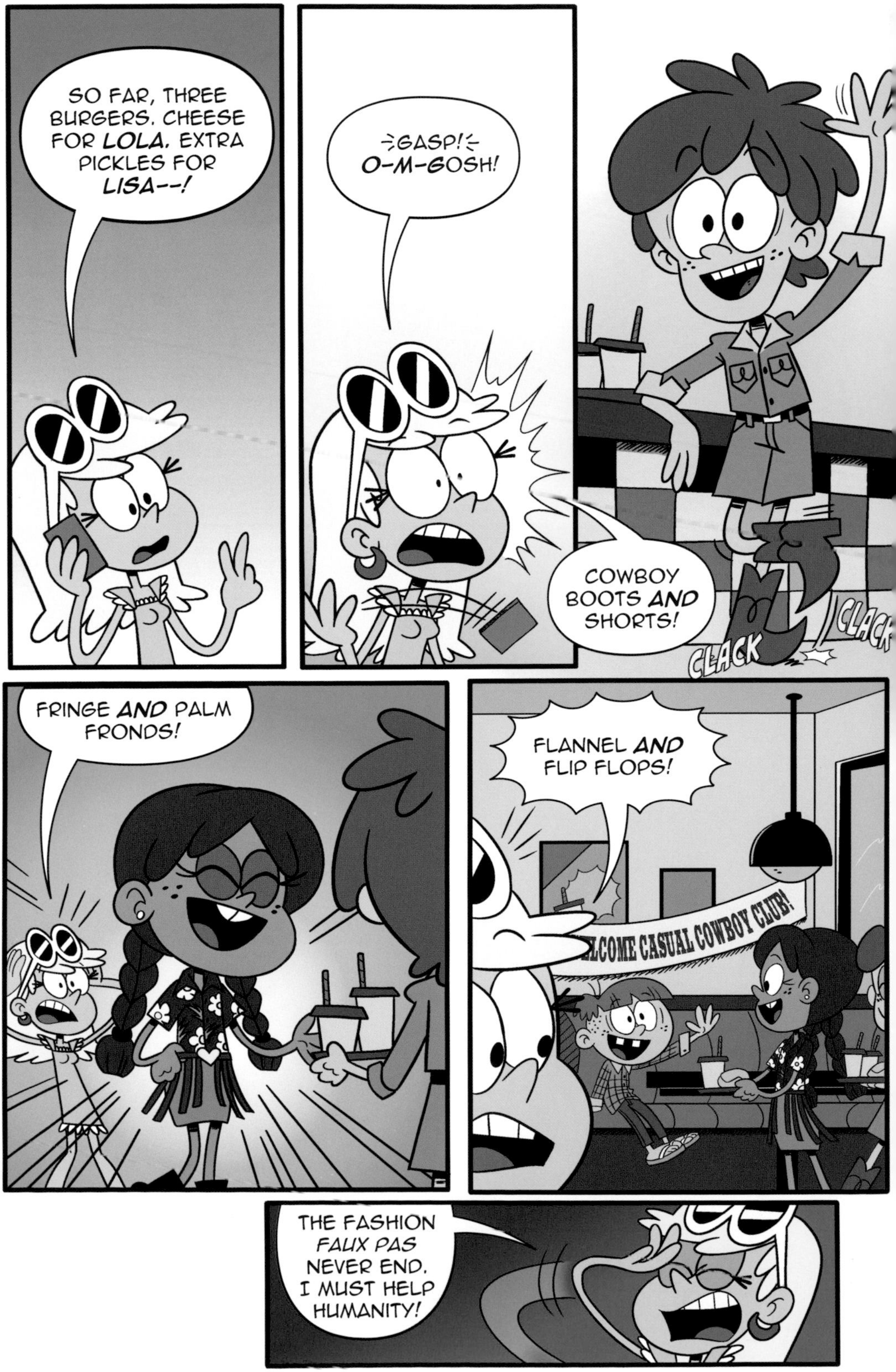
SO FAR, THREE BURGERS. CHEESE FOR LOLA. EXTRA PICKLES FOR LISA--!
GASP! O-M-GOSH!
COWBOY BOOTS AND SHORTS!
CLACK
CLACK
FRINGE AND PALM FRONDS!
FLANNEL AND FLIP FLOPS!
LCOME CASUAL COWBOY CLUB!
THE FASHION FAUX PAS NEVER END. I MUST HELP HUMANITY!

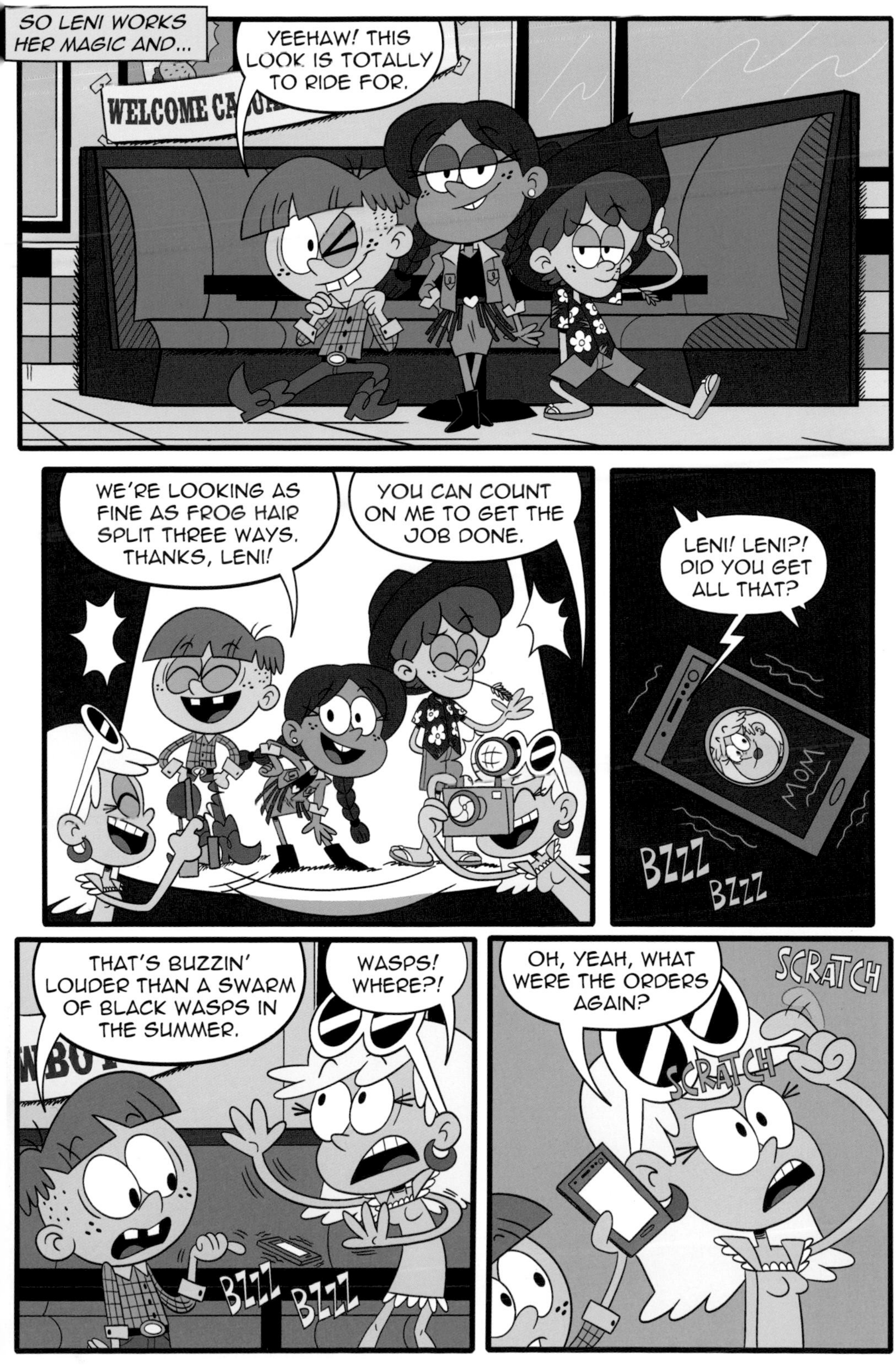
SO LENI WORKS HER MAGIC AND...
YEEHAW! THIS LOOK IS TOTALLY TO RIDE FOR.
WELCOME CA
WE'RE LOOKING AS FINE AS FROG HAIR SPLIT THREE WAYS. THANKS, LENI!
YOU CAN COUNT ON ME TO GET THE JOB DONE.
LENI! LENI?! DID YOU GET ALL THAT?
MOM
BZZZ
BZZZ
THAT'S BUZZIN' LOUDER THAN A SWARM OF BLACK WASPS IN THE SUMMER.
WASPS! WHERE?!
BZZZ
BZZZ
OH, YEAH, WHAT WERE THE ORDERS AGAIN?
SCRATCH
SCRATCH

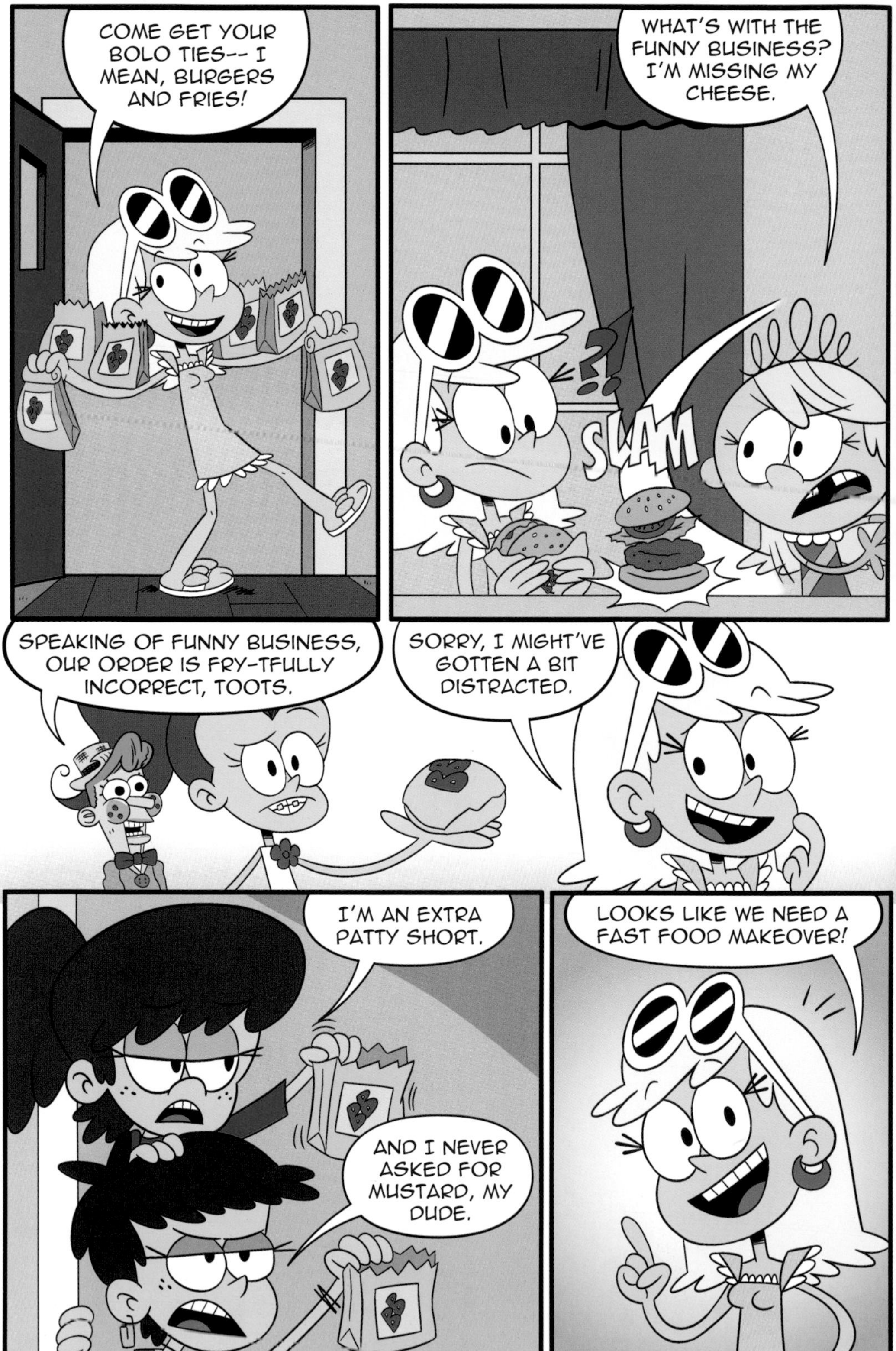
COME GET YOUR BOLO TIES-- I MEAN, BURGERS AND FRIES!
WHAT'S WITH THE FUNNY BUSINESS? I'M MISSING MY CHEESE.
?!
SLAM
SPEAKING OF FUNNY BUSINESS, OUR ORDER IS FRY-TFULLY INCORRECT, TOOTS.
SORRY, I MIGHT'VE GOTTEN A BIT DISTRACTED.
I'M AN EXTRA PATTY SHORT.
AND I NEVER ASKED FOR MUSTARD, MY DUDE.
LOOKS LIKE WE NEED A FAST FOOD MAKEOVER!

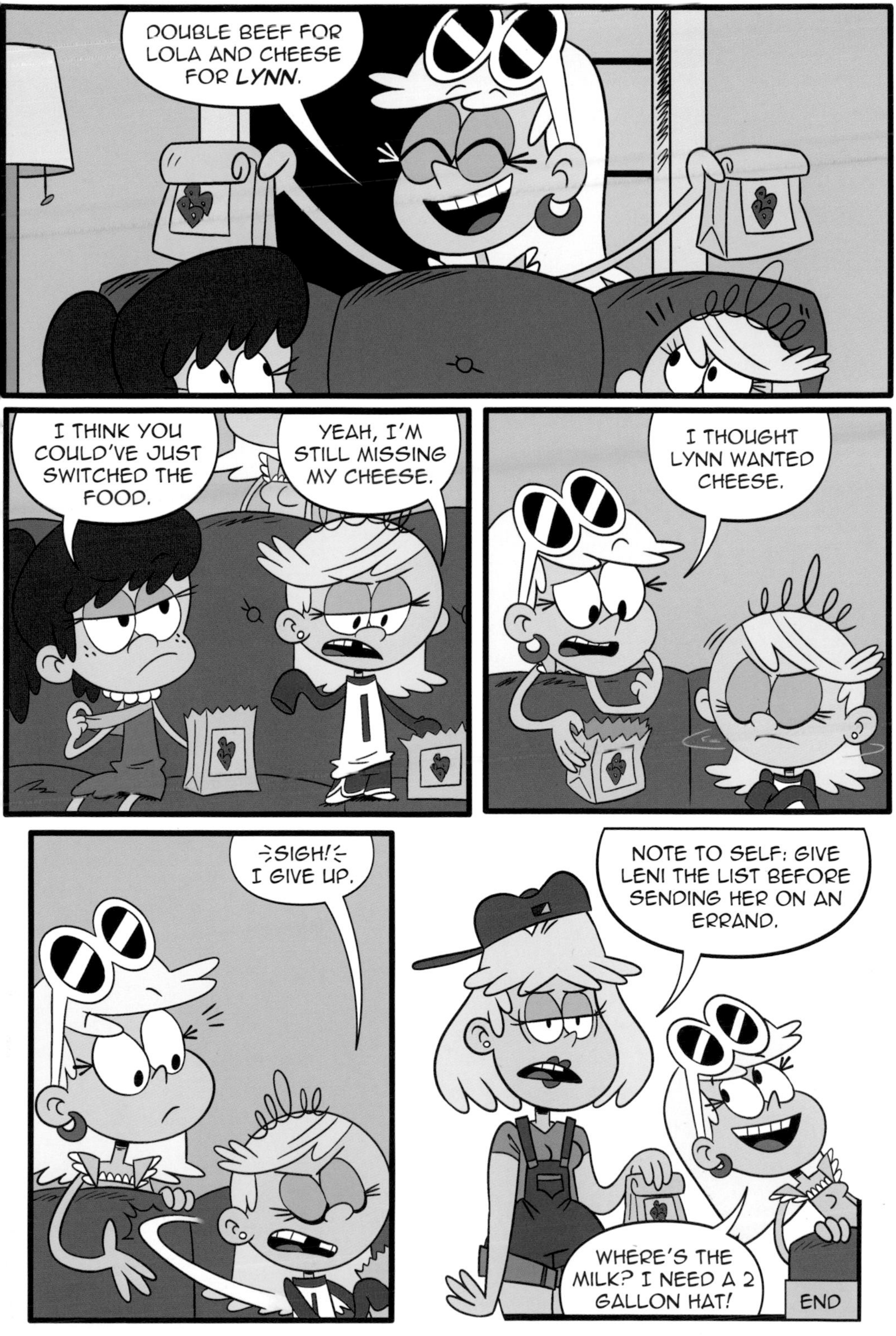

DOUBLE BEEF FOR LOLA AND CHEESE FOR LYNN.
I THINK YOU COULD'VE JUST SWITCHED THE FOOD.
YEAH, I'M STILL MISSING MY CHEESE.
I THOUGHT LYNN WANTED CHEESE.
SIGH! I GIVE UP.
NOTE TO SELF: GIVE LENI THE LIST BEFORE SENDING HER ON AN ERRAND.
WHERE'S THE MILK? I NEED A 2 GALLON HAT!
END

"BARNYARD BLUES"

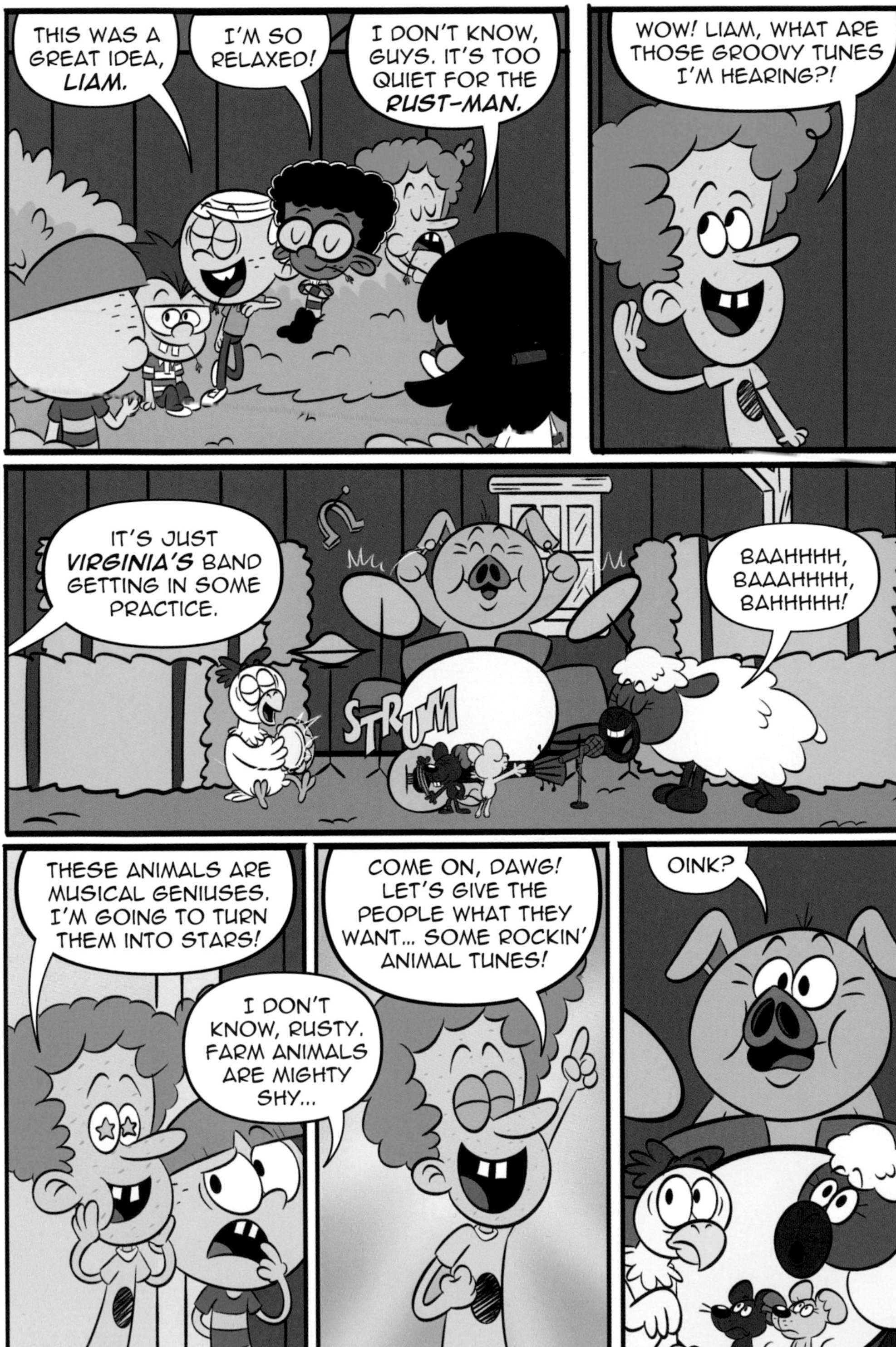
THIS WAS A GREAT IDEA, LIAM.
I'M SO RELAXED!
I DON'T KNOW, GUYS. IT'S TOO QUIET FOR THE RUST-MAN.
WOW! LIAM, WHAT ARE THOSE GROOVY TUNES I'M HEARING?!
IT'S JUST VIRGINIA'S BAND GETTING IN SOME PRACTICE.
BAAHHHH, BAAAHHHH, BAHHHHH!
STRUM
THESE ANIMALS ARE MUSICAL GENIUSES. I'M GOING TO TURN THEM INTO STARS!
I DON'T KNOW, RUSTY. FARM ANIMALS ARE MIGHTY SHY...
COME ON, DAWG! LET'S GIVE THE PEOPLE WHAT THEY WANT... SOME ROCKIN' ANIMAL TUNES!
OINK?

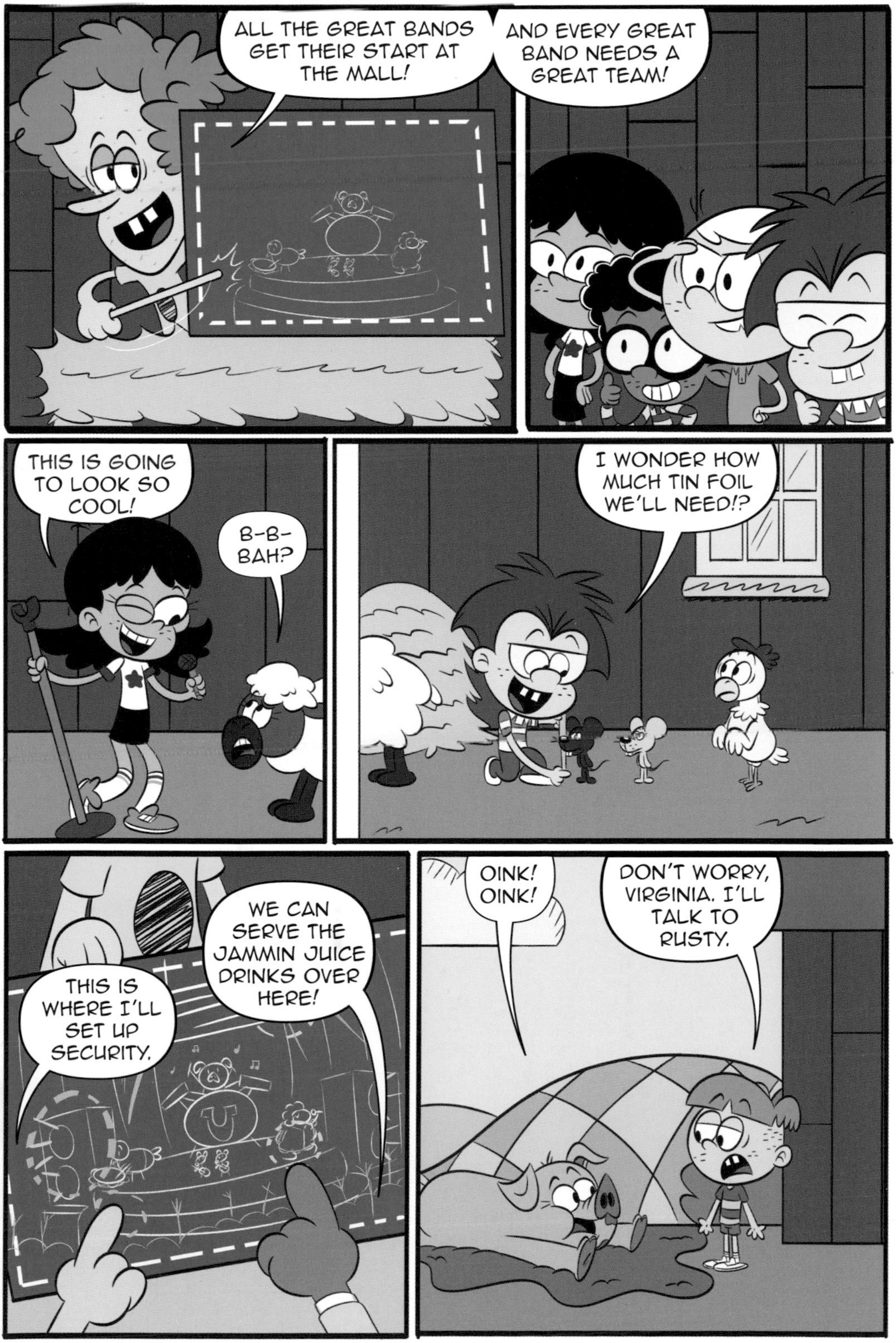
ALL THE GREAT BANDS GET THEIR START AT THE MALL!
AND EVERY GREAT BAND NEEDS A GREAT TEAM!
THIS IS GOING TO LOOK SO COOL!
B-B-BAH?
I WONDER HOW MUCH TIN FOIL WE'LL NEED!?
WE CAN SERVE THE JAMMIN JUICE DRINKS OVER HERE!
THIS IS WHERE I'LL SET UP SECURITY.
OINK! OINK!
DON'T WORRY, VIRGINIA. I'LL TALK TO RUSTY.

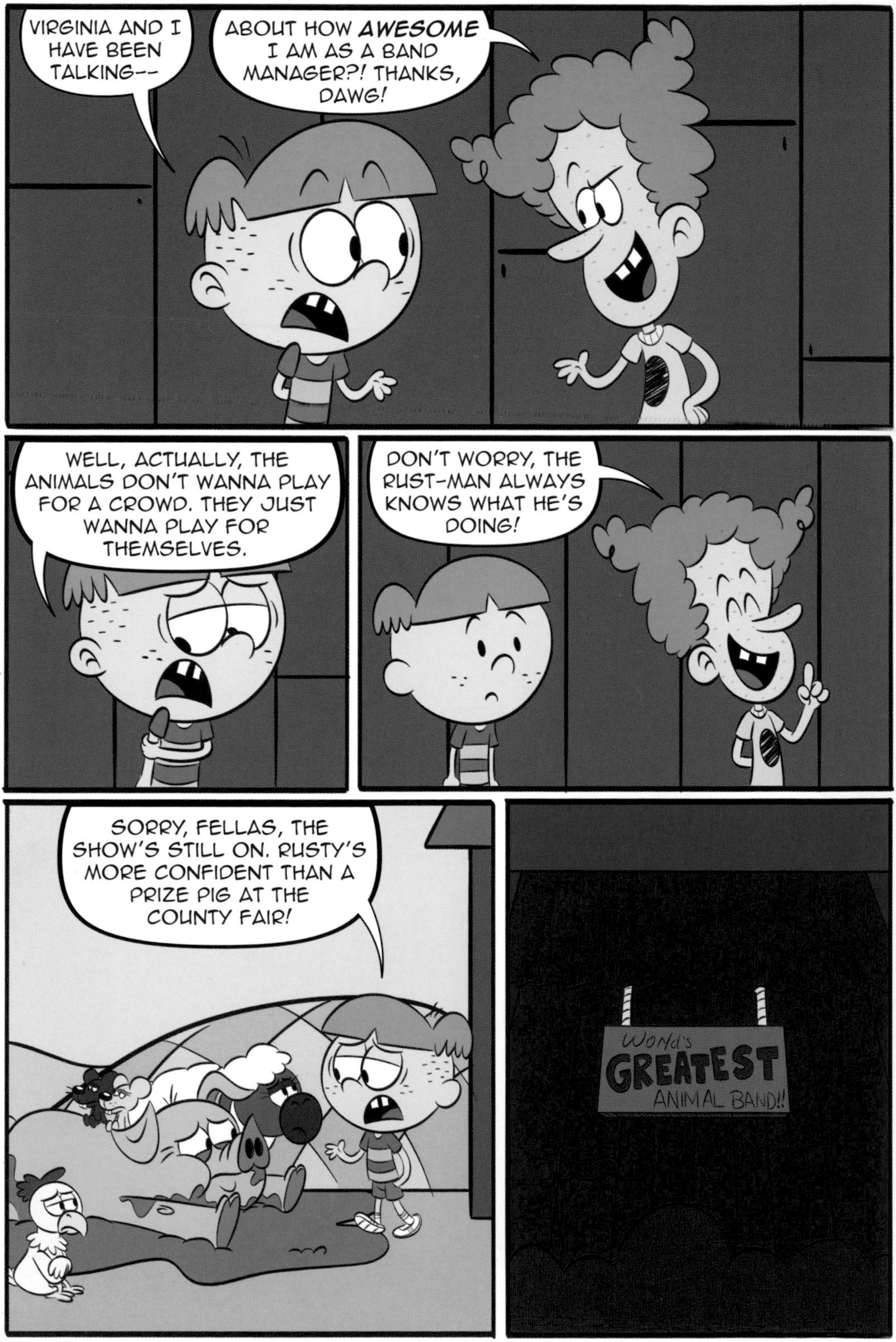
VIRGINIA AND I HAVE BEEN TALKING--
ABOUT HOW AWESOME I AM AS A BAND MANAGER?! THANKS, DAWG!
WELL, ACTUALLY, THE ANIMALS DON'T WANNA PLAY FOR A CROWD. THEY JUST WANNA PLAY FOR THEMSELVES.
DON'T WORRY, THE RUST-MAN ALWAYS KNOWS WHAT HE'S DOING!
SORRY, FELLAS, THE SHOW'S STILL ON. RUSTY'S MORE CONFIDENT THAN A PRIZE PIG AT THE COUNTY FAIR!
World's GREATEST ANIMAL BAND!!

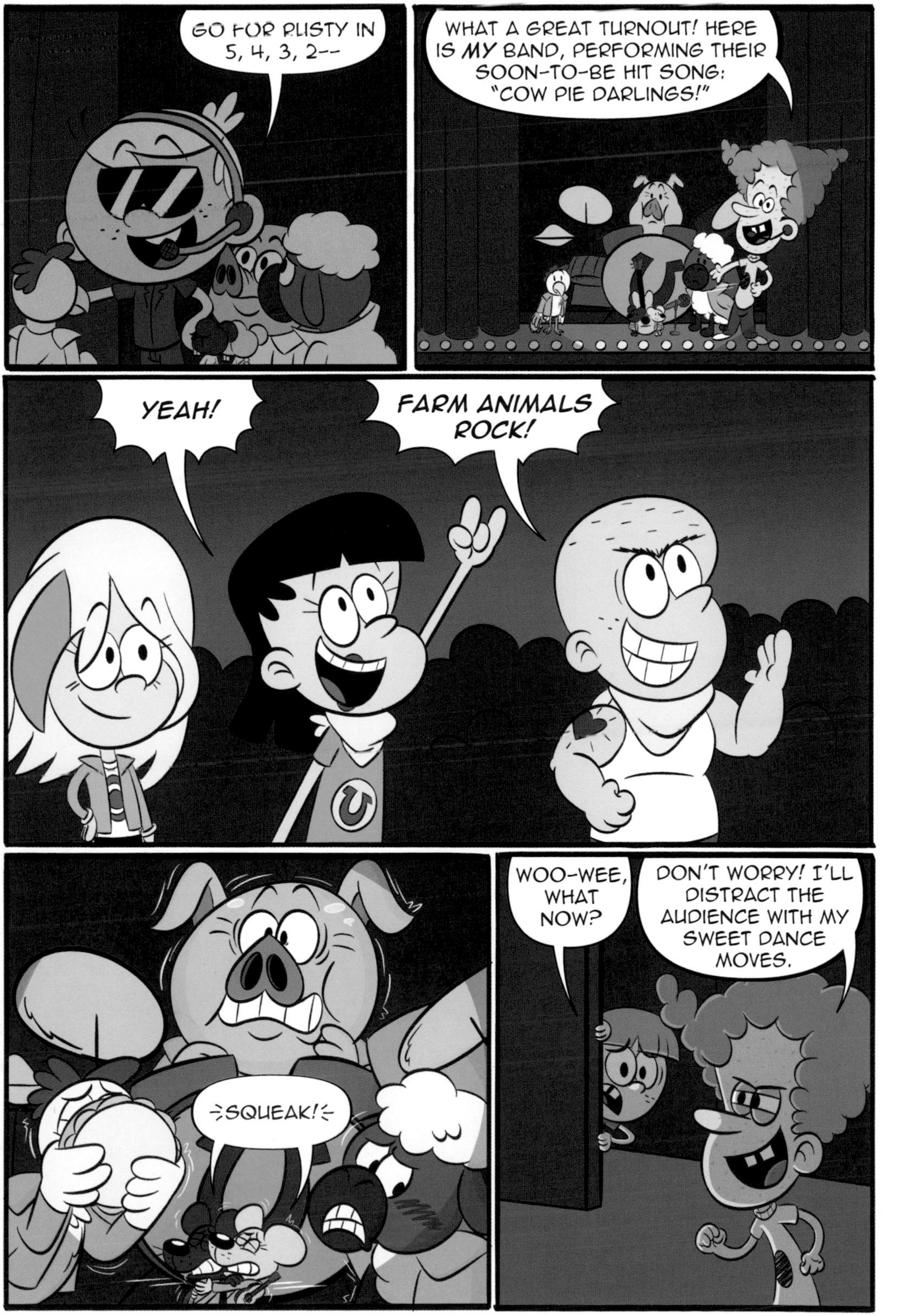
GO FOR RUSTY IN 5, 4, 3, 2--
WHAT A GREAT TURNOUT! HERE IS MY BAND, PERFORMING THEIR SOON-TO-BE HIT SONG: "COW PIE DARLINGS!"
YEAH!
FARM ANIMALS ROCK!
SQUEAK!
WOO-WEE, WHAT NOW?
DON'T WORRY! I'LL DISTRACT THE AUDIENCE WITH MY SWEET DANCE MOVES.

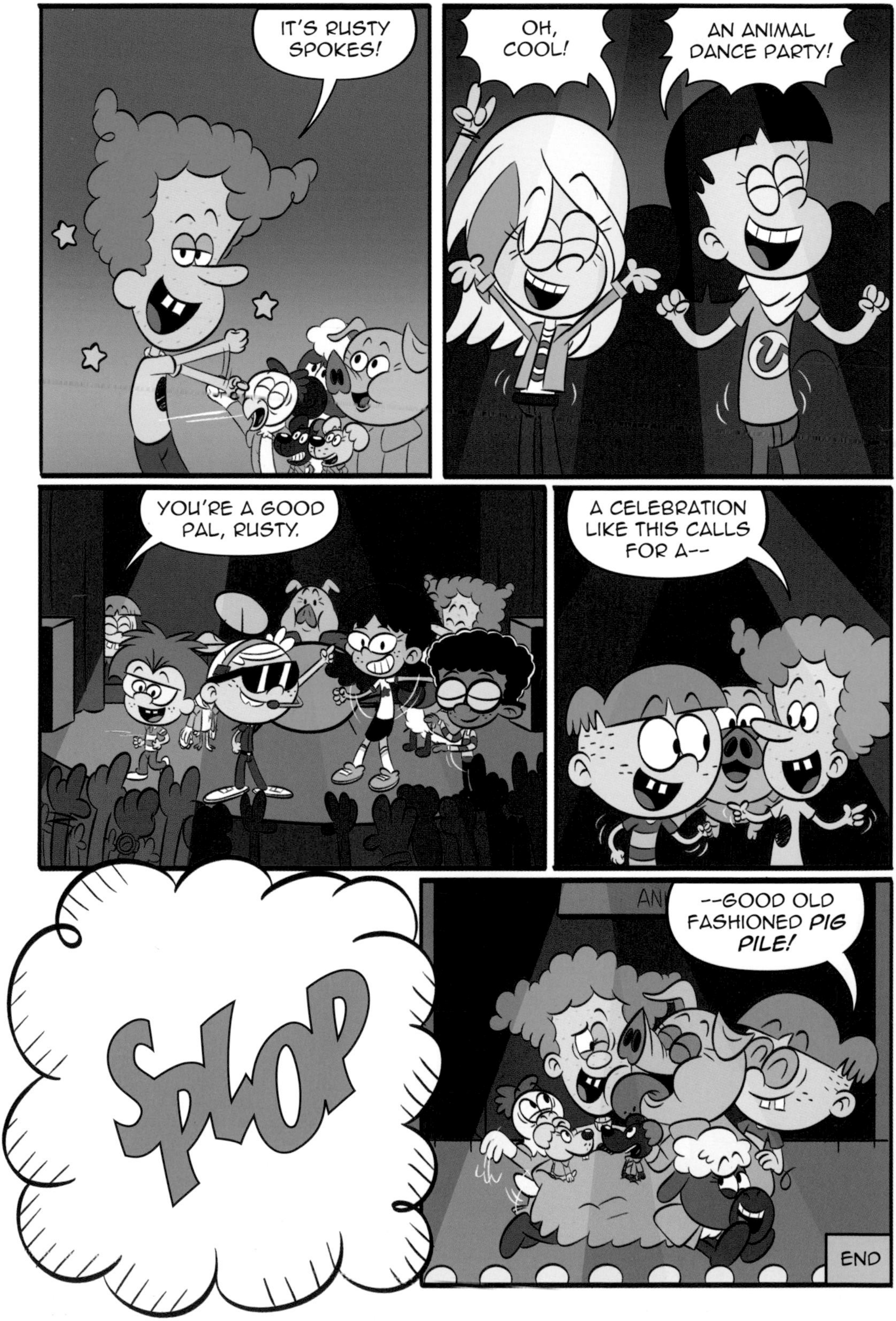
IT'S RUSTY SPOKES!
OH, COOL!
AN ANIMAL DANCE PARTY!
YOU'RE A GOOD PAL, RUSTY.
A CELEBRATION LIKE THIS CALLS FOR A--
SPLOP
--GOOD OLD FASHIONED *PIG PILE!*
END

"WHATTA DOLL"

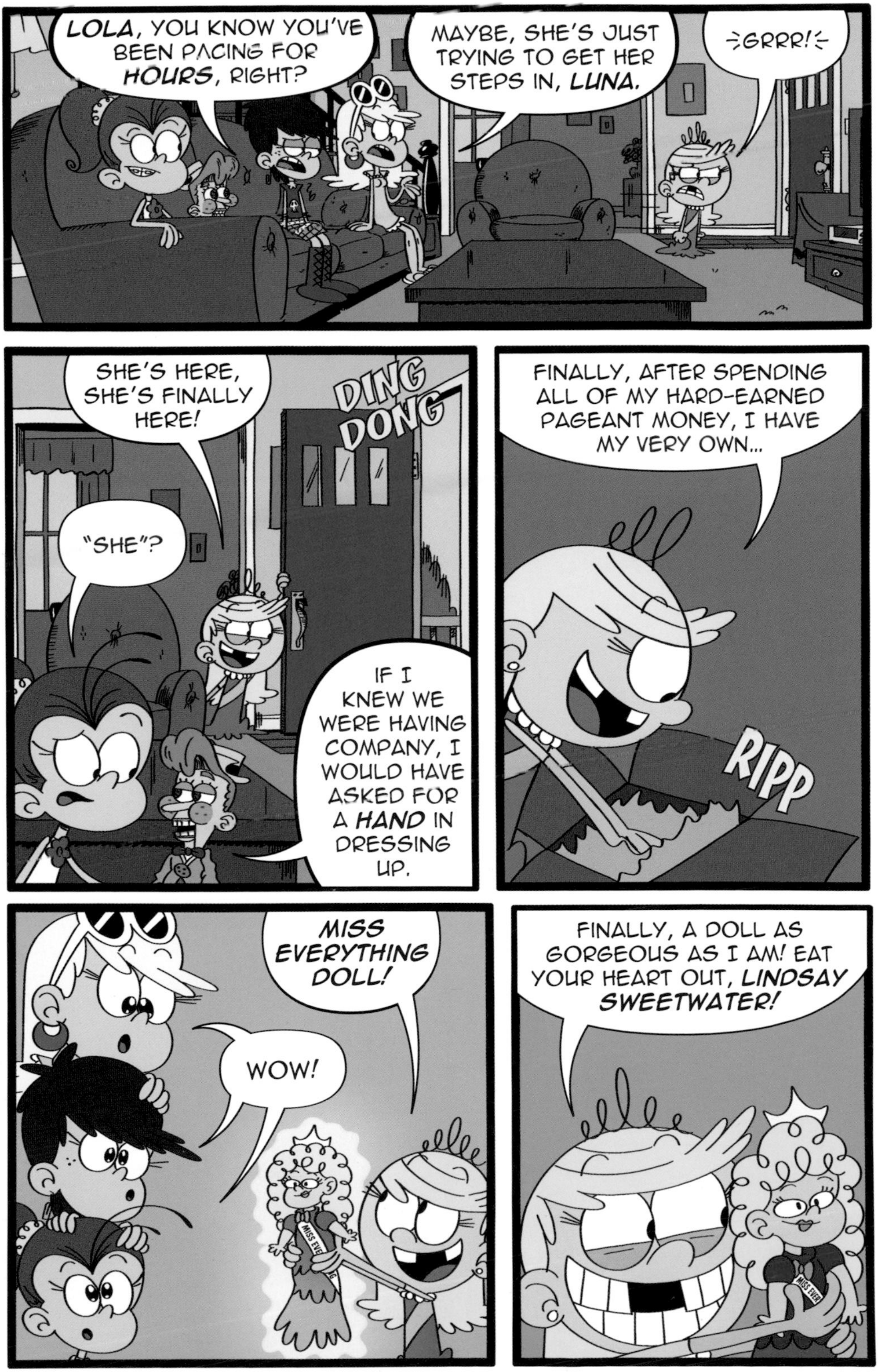

LOLA, YOU KNOW YOU'VE BEEN PACING FOR HOURS, RIGHT?
MAYBE, SHE'S JUST TRYING TO GET HER STEPS IN, LUNA.
GRRR!
SHE'S HERE, SHE'S FINALLY HERE!
DING DONG
"SHE"?
IF I KNEW WE WERE HAVING COMPANY, I WOULD HAVE ASKED FOR A HAND IN DRESSING UP.
FINALLY, AFTER SPENDING ALL OF MY HARD-EARNED PAGEANT MONEY, I HAVE MY VERY OWN...
RIPP
MISS EVERYTHING DOLL!
WOW!
FINALLY, A DOLL AS GORGEOUS AS I AM! EAT YOUR HEART OUT, LINDSAY SWEETWATER!

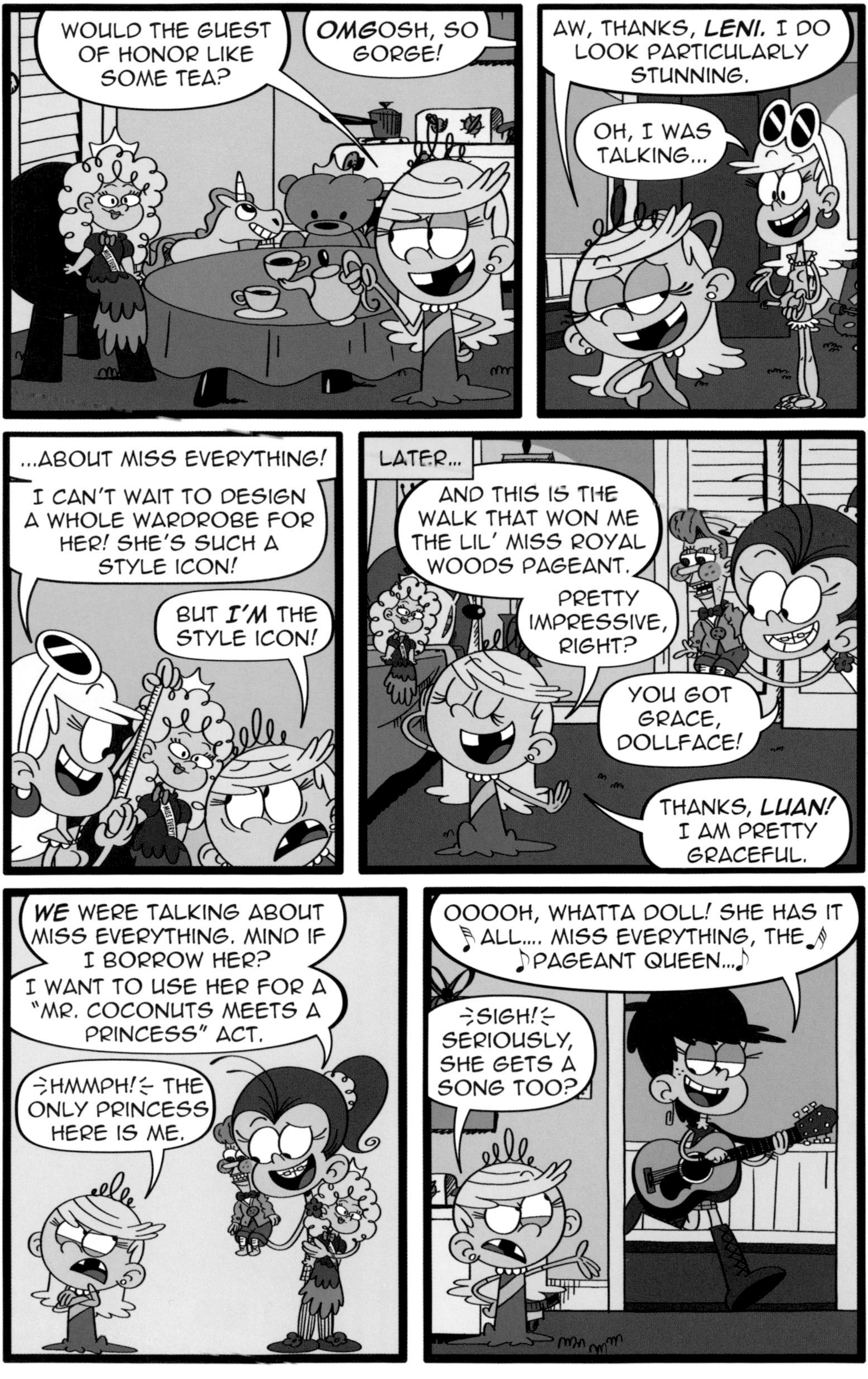
WOULD THE GUEST OF HONOR LIKE SOME TEA?
OMGOSH, SO GORGE!
AW, THANKS, LENI. I DO LOOK PARTICULARLY STUNNING.
OH, I WAS TALKING...
...ABOUT MISS EVERYTHING!
I CAN'T WAIT TO DESIGN A WHOLE WARDROBE FOR HER! SHE'S SUCH A STYLE ICON!
BUT I'M THE STYLE ICON!
LATER...
AND THIS IS THE WALK THAT WON ME THE LIL' MISS ROYAL WOODS PAGEANT.
PRETTY IMPRESSIVE, RIGHT?
YOU GOT GRACE, DOLLFACE!
THANKS, LUAN! I AM PRETTY GRACEFUL.
WE WERE TALKING ABOUT MISS EVERYTHING. MIND IF I BORROW HER?
I WANT TO USE HER FOR A "MR. COCONUTS MEETS A PRINCESS" ACT.
HMMPH! THE ONLY PRINCESS HERE IS ME.
OOOOH, WHATTA DOLL! SHE HAS IT ALL.... MISS EVERYTHING, THE PAGEANT QUEEN...
SIGH! SERIOUSLY, SHE GETS A SONG TOO?

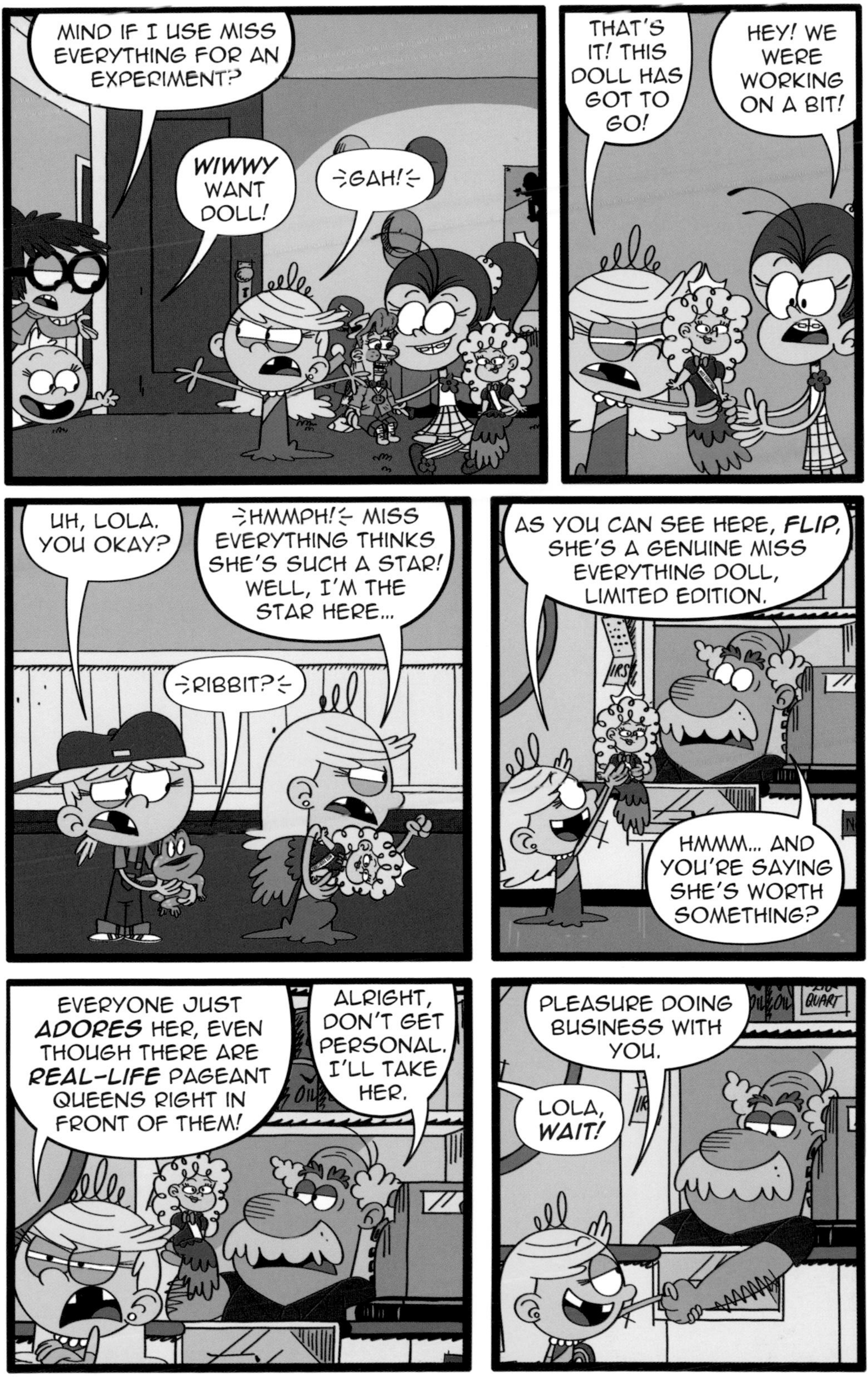
MIND IF I USE MISS EVERYTHING FOR AN EXPERIMENT?
WIWWY WANT DOLL!
GAH!
THAT'S IT! THIS DOLL HAS GOT TO GO!
HEY! WE WERE WORKING ON A BIT!
UH, LOLA. YOU OKAY?
HMMPH! MISS EVERYTHING THINKS SHE'S SUCH A STAR! WELL, I'M THE STAR HERE...
RIBBIT?
AS YOU CAN SEE HERE, FLIP, SHE'S A GENUINE MISS EVERYTHING DOLL, LIMITED EDITION.
HMMM... AND YOU'RE SAYING SHE'S WORTH SOMETHING?
EVERYONE JUST ADORES HER, EVEN THOUGH THERE ARE REAL-LIFE PAGEANT QUEENS RIGHT IN FRONT OF THEM!
ALRIGHT, DON'T GET PERSONAL. I'LL TAKE HER.
PLEASURE DOING BUSINESS WITH YOU.
LOLA, WAIT!

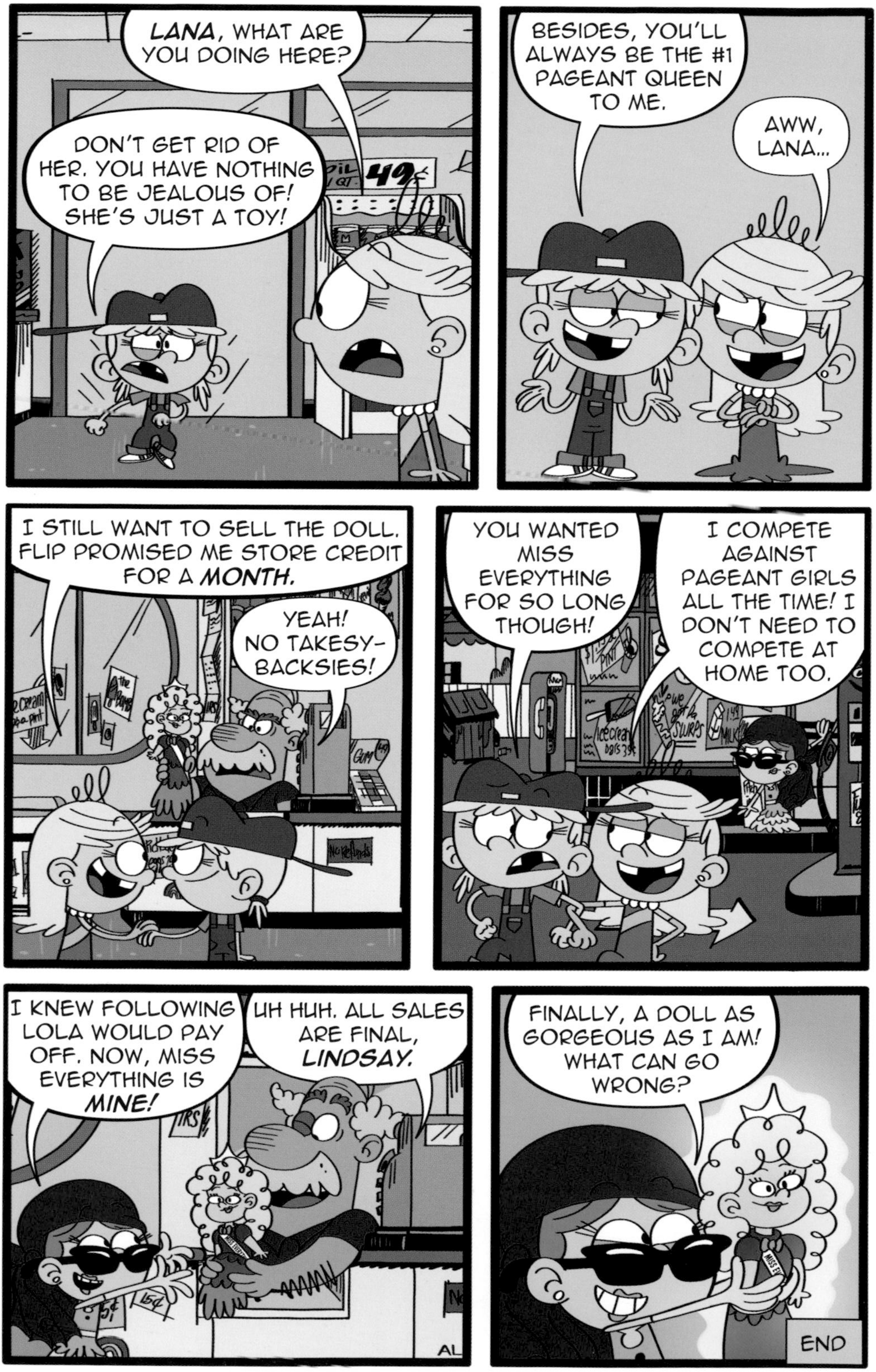
LANA, WHAT ARE YOU DOING HERE?
DON'T GET RID OF HER. YOU HAVE NOTHING TO BE JEALOUS OF! SHE'S JUST A TOY!
BESIDES, YOU'LL ALWAYS BE THE #1 PAGEANT QUEEN TO ME.
AWW, LANA...
I STILL WANT TO SELL THE DOLL. FLIP PROMISED ME STORE CREDIT FOR A MONTH.
YEAH! NO TAKESY-BACKSIES!
YOU WANTED MISS EVERYTHING FOR SO LONG THOUGH!
I COMPETE AGAINST PAGEANT GIRLS ALL THE TIME! I DON'T NEED TO COMPETE AT HOME TOO.
I KNEW FOLLOWING LOLA WOULD PAY OFF. NOW, MISS EVERYTHING IS MINE!
UH HUH. ALL SALES ARE FINAL, LINDSAY.
FINALLY, A DOLL AS GORGEOUS AS I AM! WHAT CAN GO WRONG?
END

"IT'S ALIVE!"

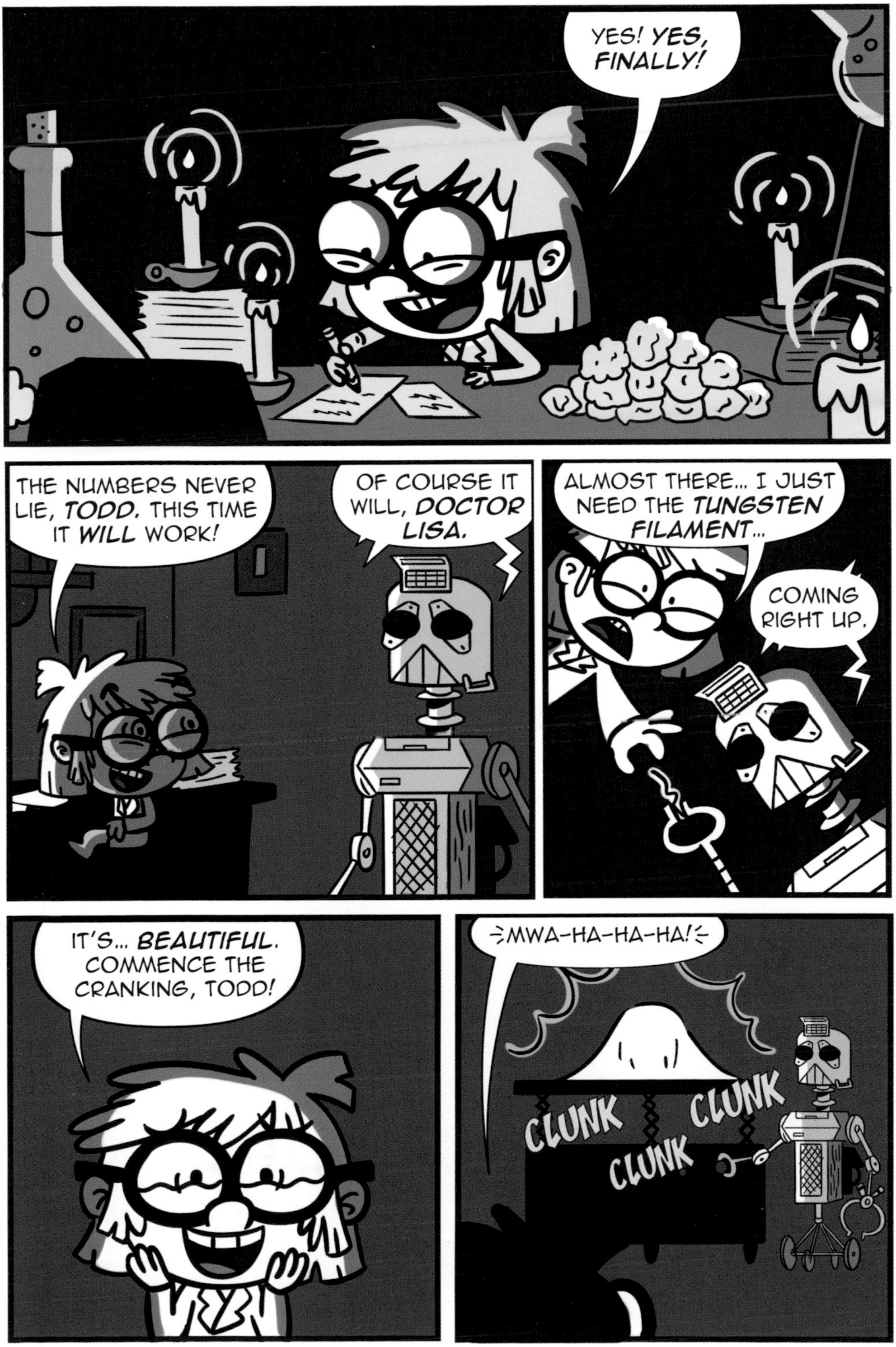

YES! YES, FINALLY!
THE NUMBERS NEVER LIE, TODD. THIS TIME IT WILL WORK!
OF COURSE IT WILL, DOCTOR LISA.
ALMOST THERE... I JUST NEED THE TUNGSTEN FILAMENT...
COMING RIGHT UP.
IT'S... BEAUTIFUL. COMMENCE THE CRANKING, TODD!
MWA-HA-HA-HA!
CLUNK
CLUNK
CLUNK

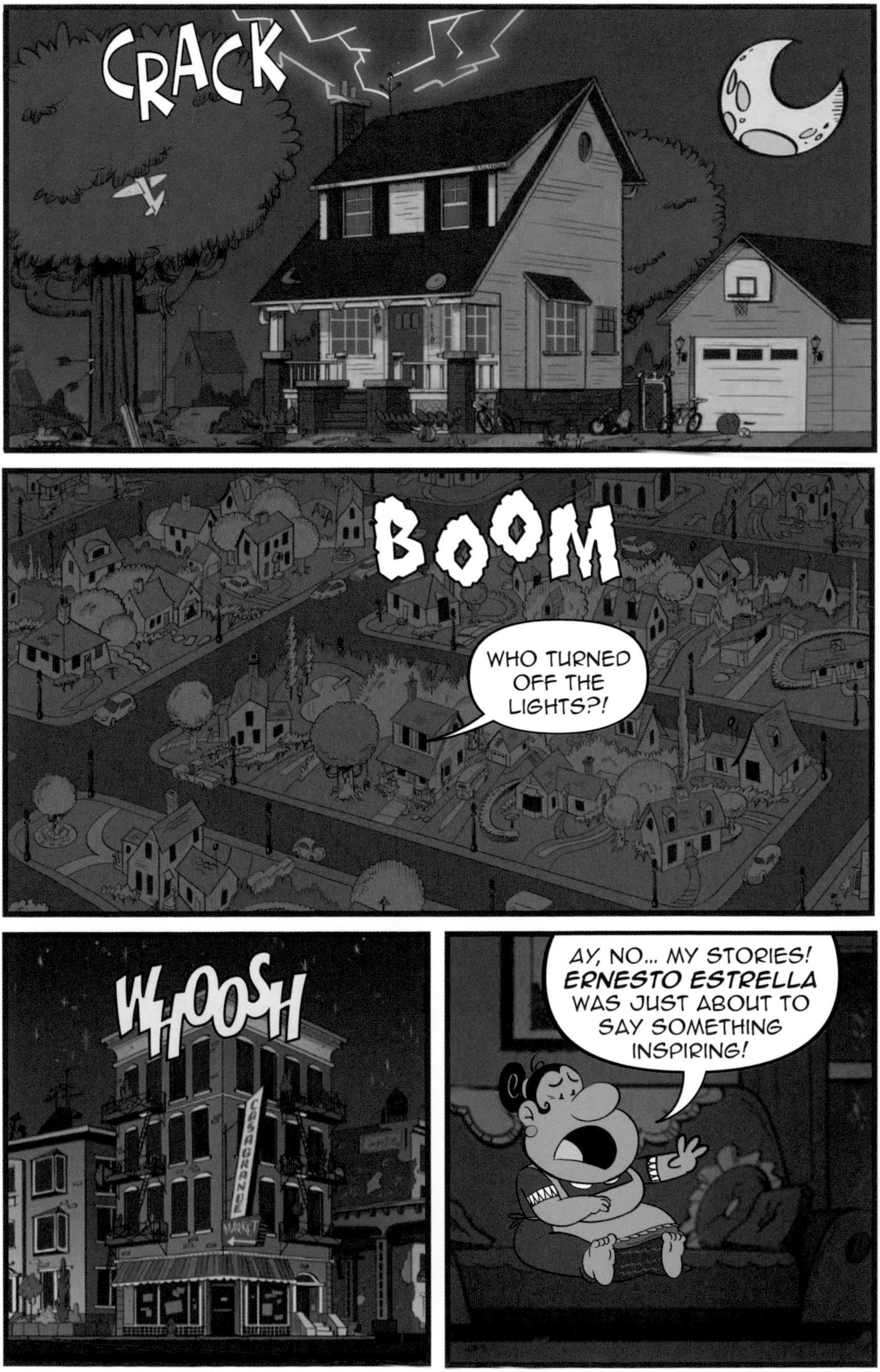
CRACK
BOOM
WHO TURNED OFF THE LIGHTS?!
WHOOSH
CASAGRANDE
MARKET
AY, NO... MY STORIES! ***ERNESTO ESTRELLA*** WAS JUST ABOUT TO SAY SOMETHING INSPIRING!

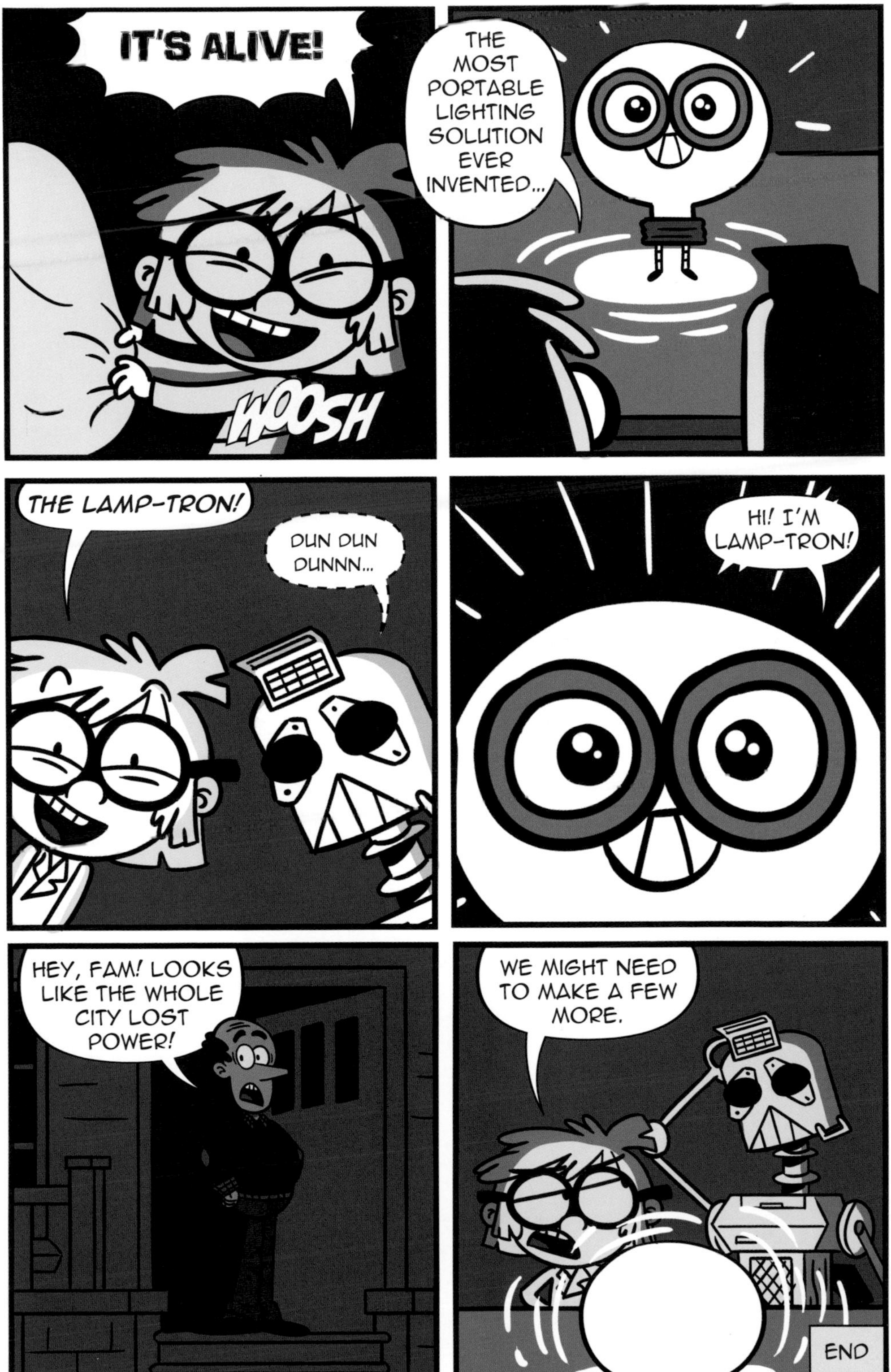
IT'S ALIVE!
WOOSH
THE MOST PORTABLE LIGHTING SOLUTION EVER INVENTED...
THE LAMP-TRON!
DUN DUN DUNNN...
HI! I'M LAMP-TRON!
HEY, FAM! LOOKS LIKE THE WHOLE CITY LOST POWER!
WE MIGHT NEED TO MAKE A FEW MORE.
END

"FOR-GOAT-TEN RECIPE"

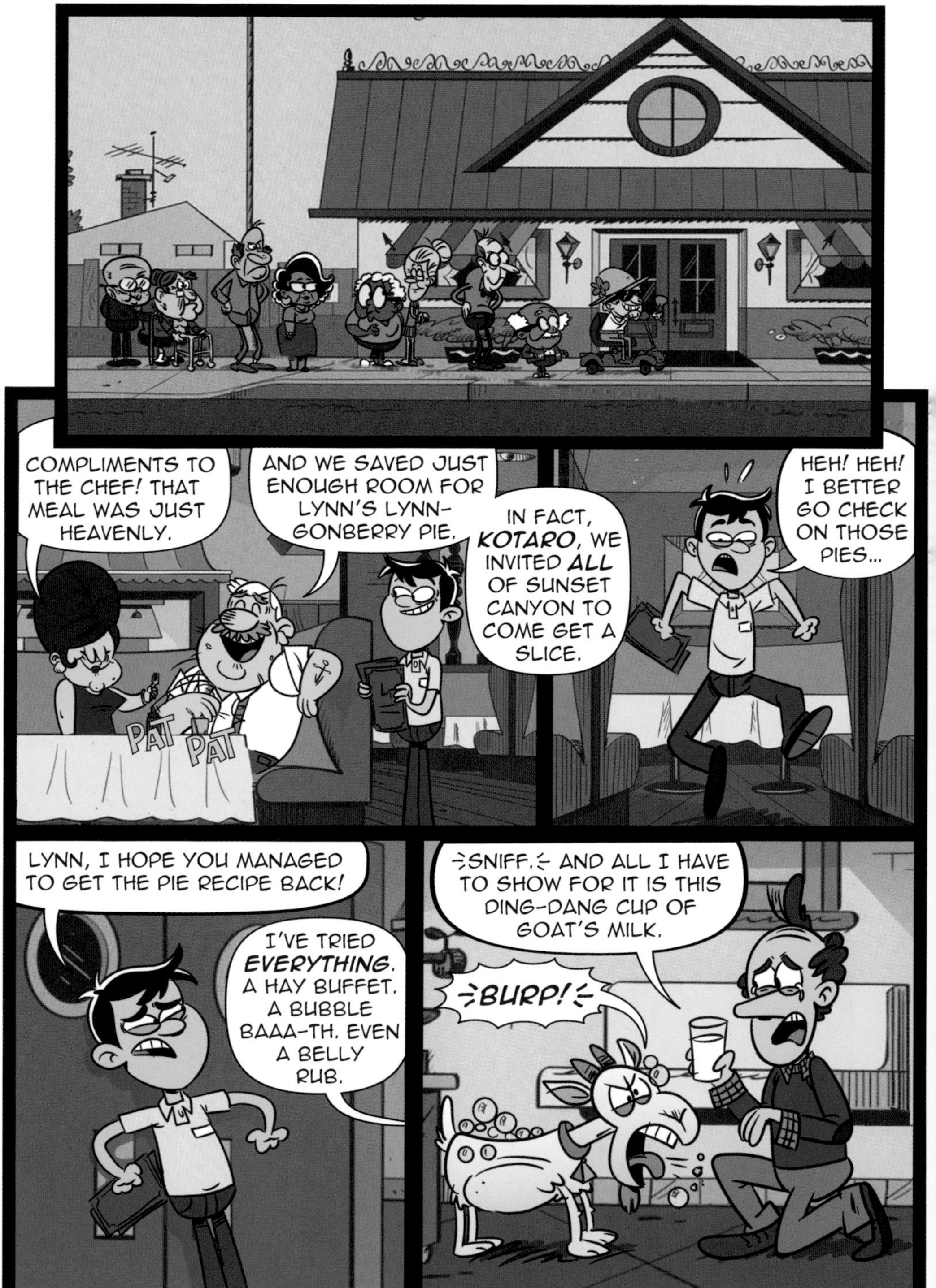
COMPLIMENTS TO THE CHEF! THAT MEAL WAS JUST HEAVENLY.
PAT PAT
AND WE SAVED JUST ENOUGH ROOM FOR LYNN'S LYNN-GONBERRY PIE.
IN FACT, KOTARO, WE INVITED ALL OF SUNSET CANYON TO COME GET A SLICE.
HEH! HEH! I BETTER GO CHECK ON THOSE PIES...
LYNN, I HOPE YOU MANAGED TO GET THE PIE RECIPE BACK!
I'VE TRIED EVERYTHING. A HAY BUFFET. A BUBBLE BAAA-TH. EVEN A BELLY RUB.
SNIFF. AND ALL I HAVE TO SHOW FOR IT IS THIS DING-DANG CUP OF GOAT'S MILK.
BURP!

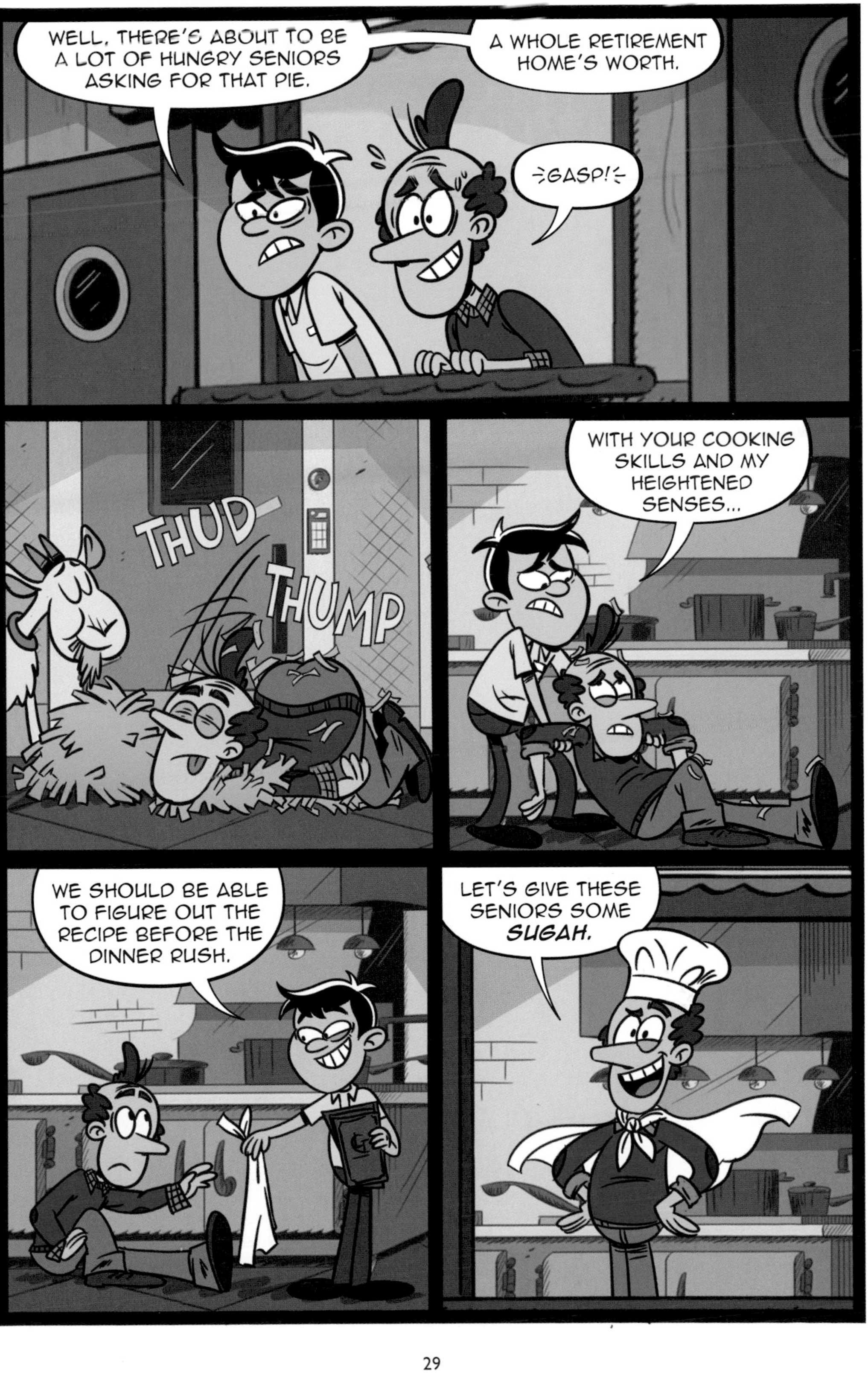
WELL, THERE'S ABOUT TO BE A LOT OF HUNGRY SENIORS ASKING FOR THAT PIE.
A WHOLE RETIREMENT HOME'S WORTH.
GASP!
THUD
THUMP
WITH YOUR COOKING SKILLS AND MY HEIGHTENED SENSES...
WE SHOULD BE ABLE TO FIGURE OUT THE RECIPE BEFORE THE DINNER RUSH.
LET'S GIVE THESE SENIORS SOME *SUGAH.*

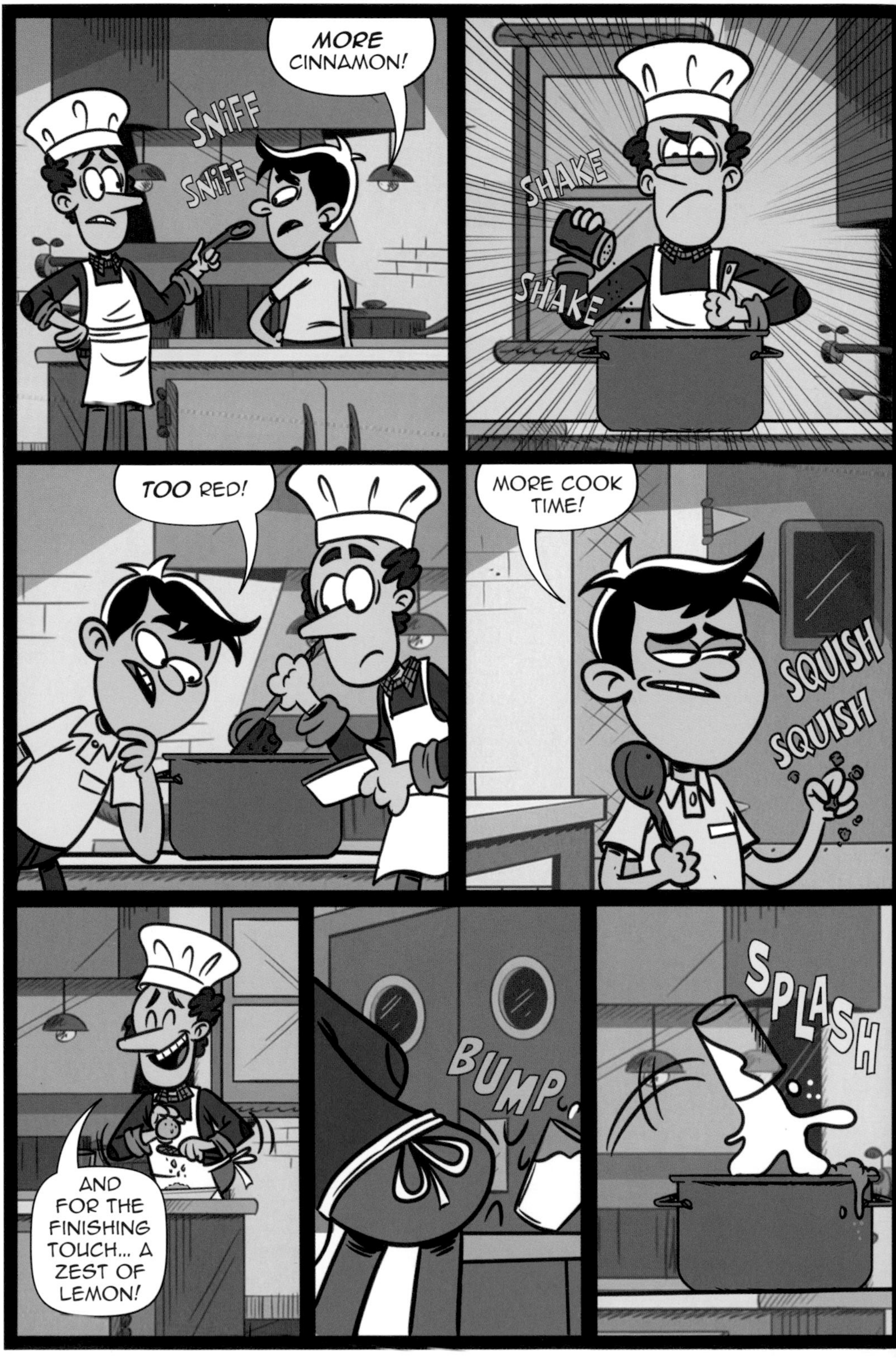
MORE CINNAMON!
SNIFF
SNIFF
SHAKE
SHAKE
TOO RED!
MORE COOK TIME!
SQUISH
SQUISH
AND FOR THE FINISHING TOUCH... A ZEST OF LEMON!
BUMP
SPLASH

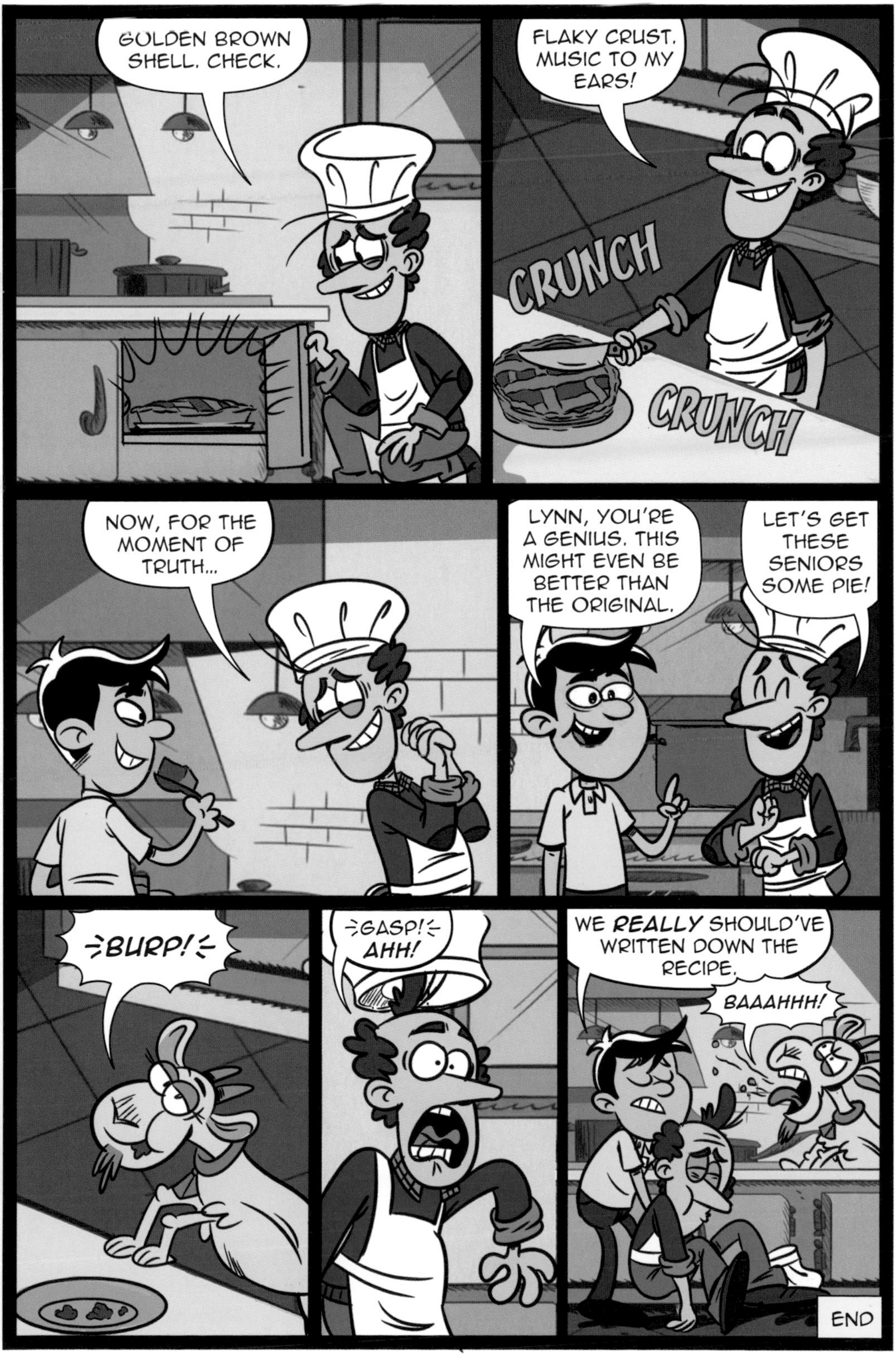
GOLDEN BROWN SHELL. CHECK.
FLAKY CRUST. MUSIC TO MY EARS!
CRUNCH
CRUNCH
NOW, FOR THE MOMENT OF TRUTH...
LYNN, YOU'RE A GENIUS. THIS MIGHT EVEN BE BETTER THAN THE ORIGINAL.
LET'S GET THESE SENIORS SOME PIE!
BURP!
GASP!
AHH!
WE REALLY SHOULD'VE WRITTEN DOWN THE RECIPE.
BAAAHHH!
END

"MEE MAWLICE"

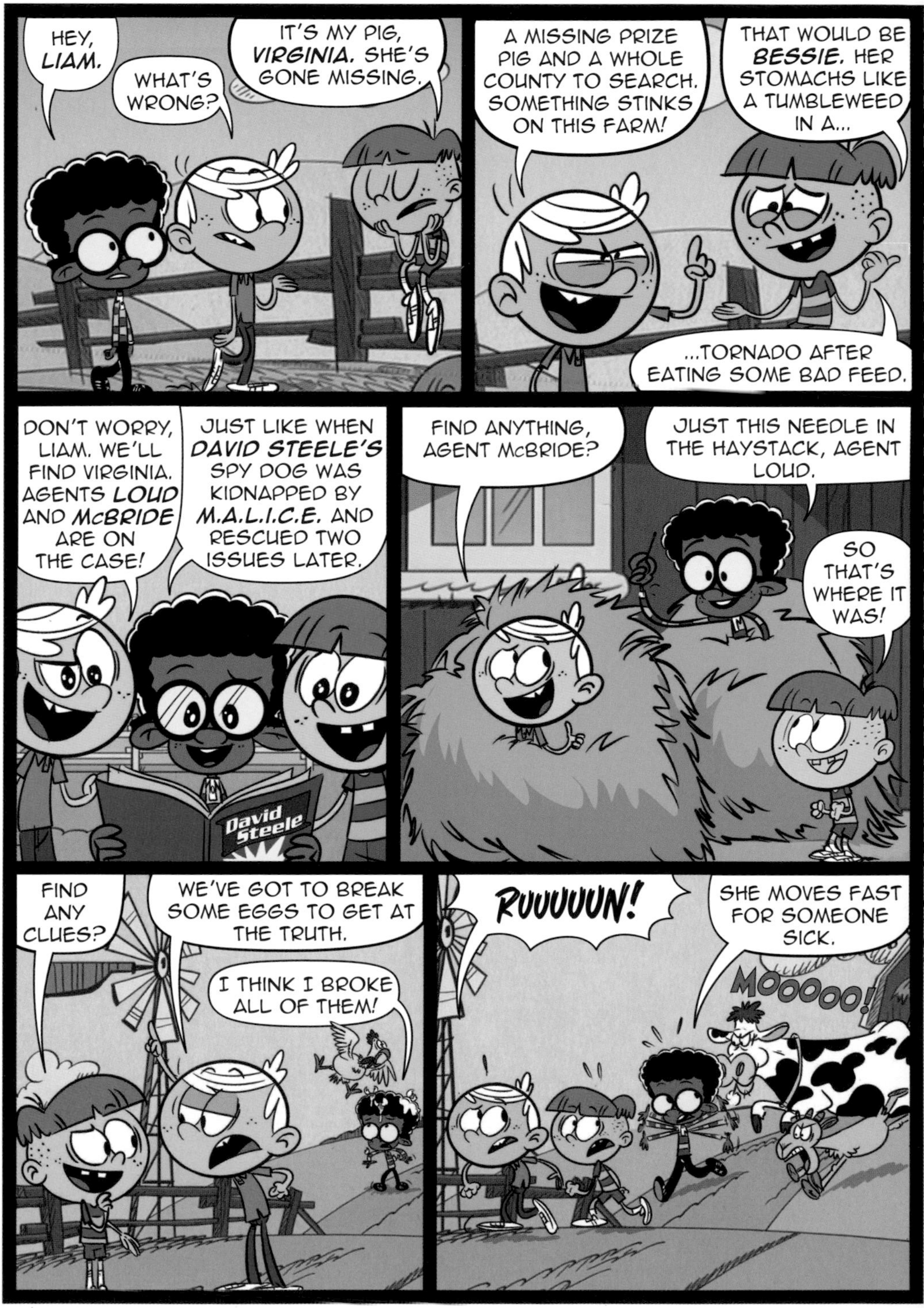
HEY, LIAM.
WHAT'S WRONG?
IT'S MY PIG, VIRGINIA. SHE'S GONE MISSING.
A MISSING PRIZE PIG AND A WHOLE COUNTY TO SEARCH. SOMETHING STINKS ON THIS FARM!
THAT WOULD BE BESSIE. HER STOMACHS LIKE A TUMBLEWEED IN A...
...TORNADO AFTER EATING SOME BAD FEED.
DON'T WORRY, LIAM. WE'LL FIND VIRGINIA. AGENTS LOUD AND McBRIDE ARE ON THE CASE!
JUST LIKE WHEN DAVID STEELE'S SPY DOG WAS KIDNAPPED BY M.A.L.I.C.E. AND RESCUED TWO ISSUES LATER.
David Steele
FIND ANYTHING, AGENT McBRIDE?
JUST THIS NEEDLE IN THE HAYSTACK, AGENT LOUD.
SO THAT'S WHERE IT WAS!
FIND ANY CLUES?
WE'VE GOT TO BREAK SOME EGGS TO GET AT THE TRUTH.
I THINK I BROKE ALL OF THEM!
RUUUUUN!
SHE MOVES FAST FOR SOMEONE SICK.
MOOOOO!

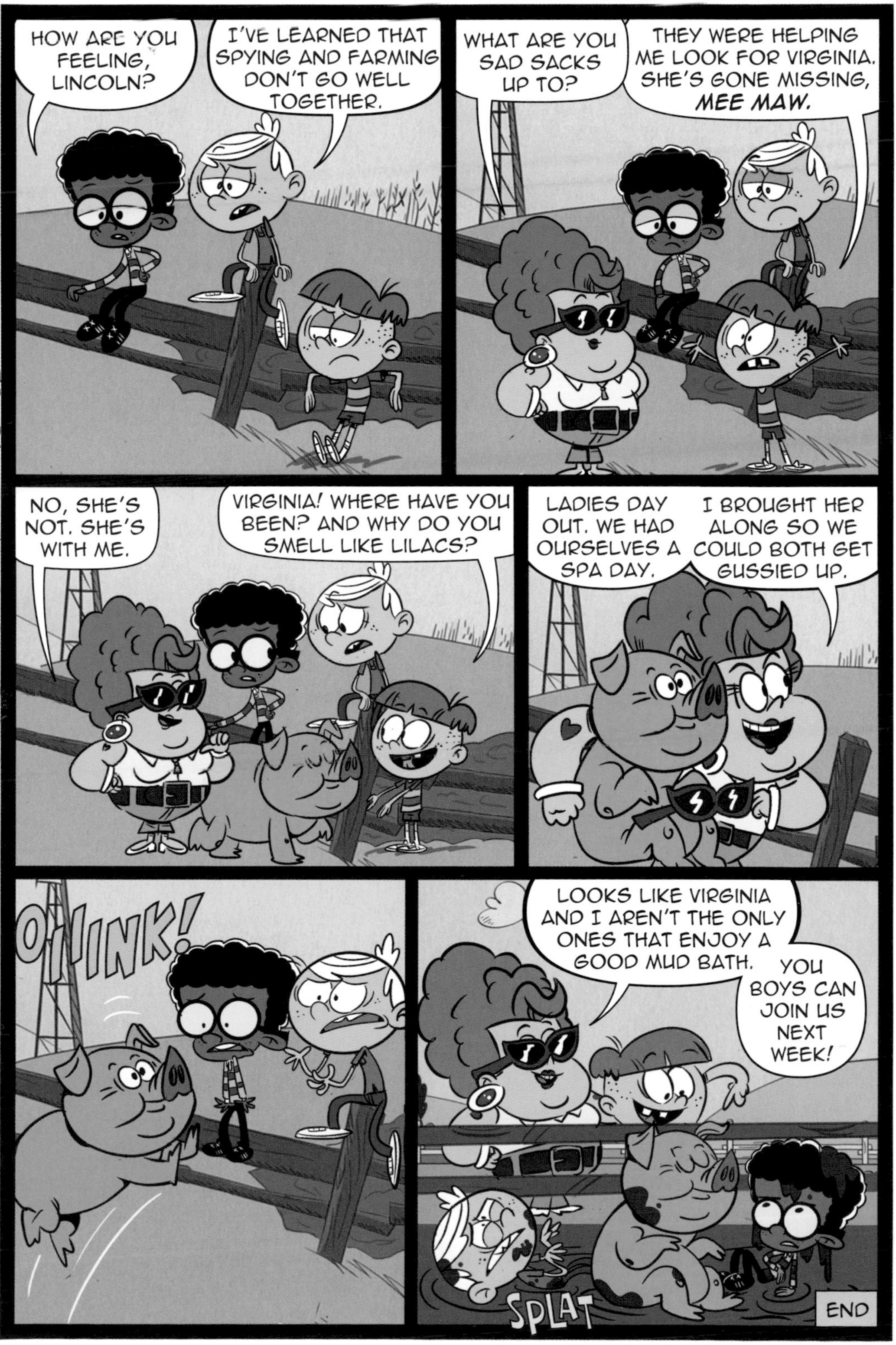
HOW ARE YOU FEELING, LINCOLN?
I'VE LEARNED THAT SPYING AND FARMING DON'T GO WELL TOGETHER.
WHAT ARE YOU SAD SACKS UP TO?
THEY WERE HELPING ME LOOK FOR VIRGINIA. SHE'S GONE MISSING, MEE MAW.
NO, SHE'S NOT. SHE'S WITH ME.
VIRGINIA! WHERE HAVE YOU BEEN? AND WHY DO YOU SMELL LIKE LILACS?
LADIES DAY OUT. WE HAD OURSELVES A SPA DAY.
I BROUGHT HER ALONG SO WE COULD BOTH GET GUSSIED UP.
OIIINK!
LOOKS LIKE VIRGINIA AND I AREN'T THE ONLY ONES THAT ENJOY A GOOD MUD BATH.
YOU BOYS CAN JOIN US NEXT WEEK!
SPLAT
END

"FLIP'S FLOPS"

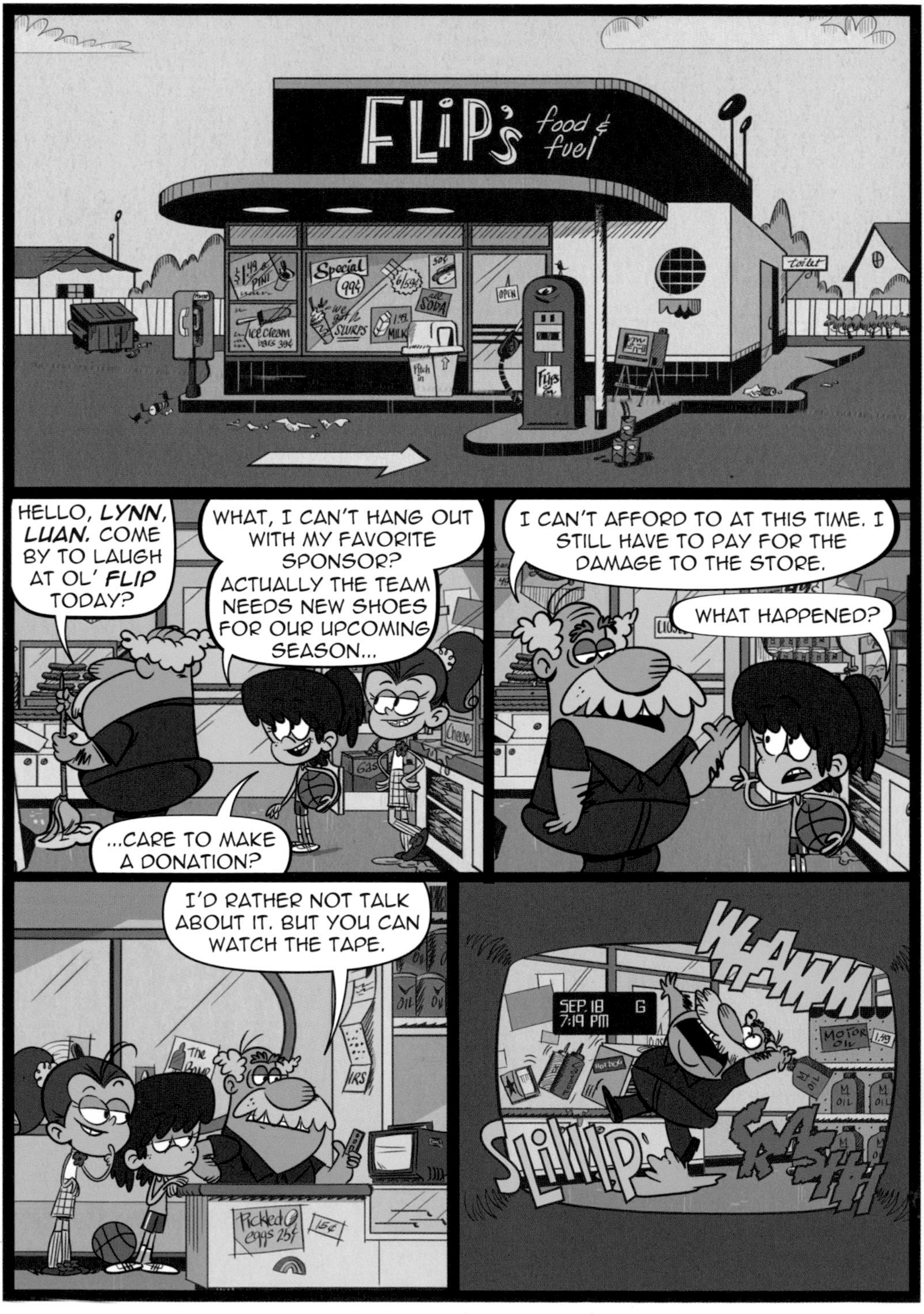
FLiP's food & fuel
HELLO, LYNN, LUAN. COME BY TO LAUGH AT OL' FLIP TODAY?
WHAT, I CAN'T HANG OUT WITH MY FAVORITE SPONSOR? ACTUALLY THE TEAM NEEDS NEW SHOES FOR OUR UPCOMING SEASON...
...CARE TO MAKE A DONATION?
I CAN'T AFFORD TO AT THIS TIME. I STILL HAVE TO PAY FOR THE DAMAGE TO THE STORE.
WHAT HAPPENED?
I'D RATHER NOT TALK ABOUT IT. BUT YOU CAN WATCH THE TAPE.
SEP. 18 G
7:19 PM
WHAMM
SLIIIIP
CRASH

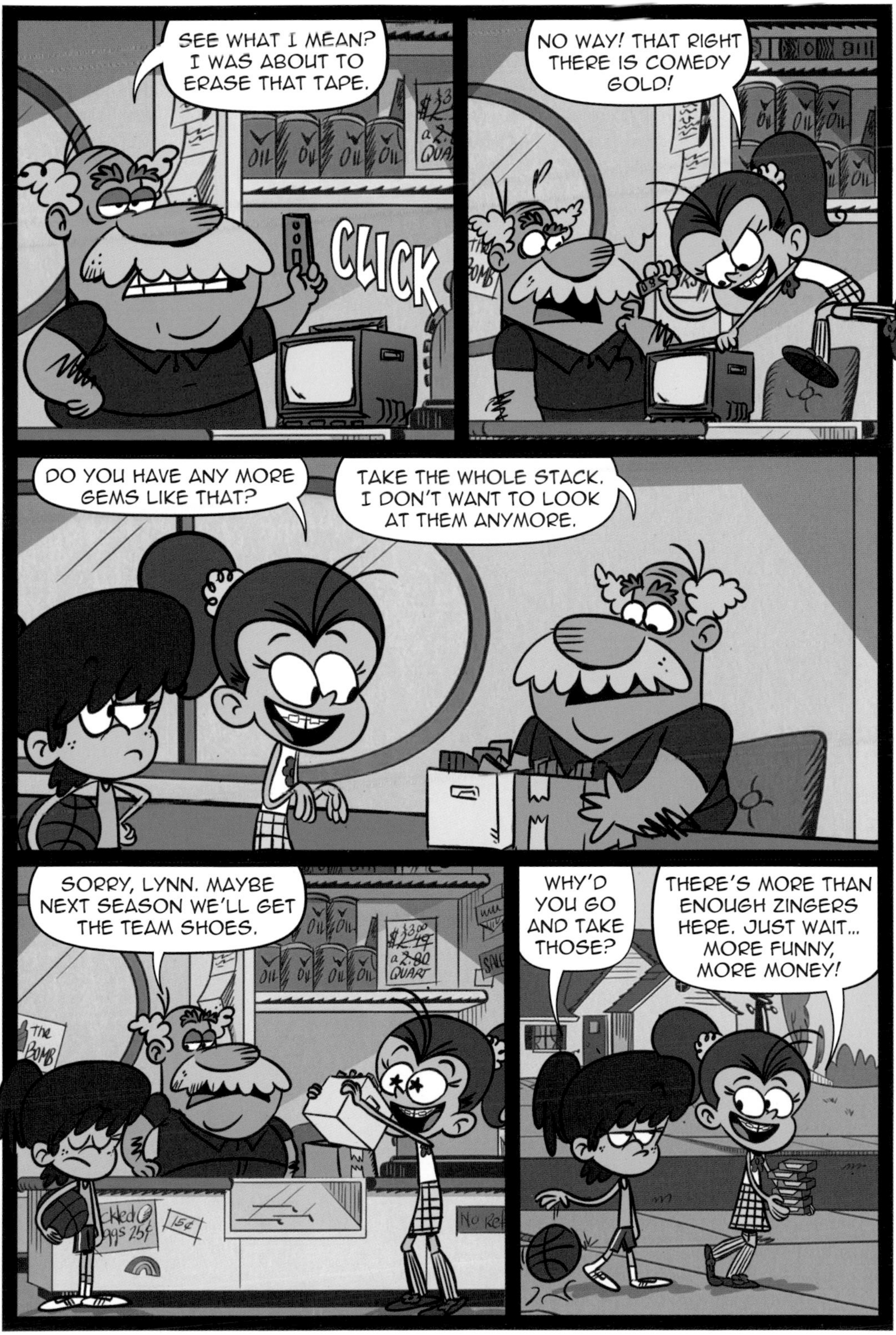
SEE WHAT I MEAN? I WAS ABOUT TO ERASE THAT TAPE.
CLICK
NO WAY! THAT RIGHT THERE IS COMEDY GOLD!
DO YOU HAVE ANY MORE GEMS LIKE THAT?
TAKE THE WHOLE STACK. I DON'T WANT TO LOOK AT THEM ANYMORE.
SORRY, LYNN. MAYBE NEXT SEASON WE'LL GET THE TEAM SHOES.
WHY'D YOU GO AND TAKE THOSE?
THERE'S MORE THAN ENOUGH ZINGERS HERE. JUST WAIT... MORE FUNNY, MORE MONEY!

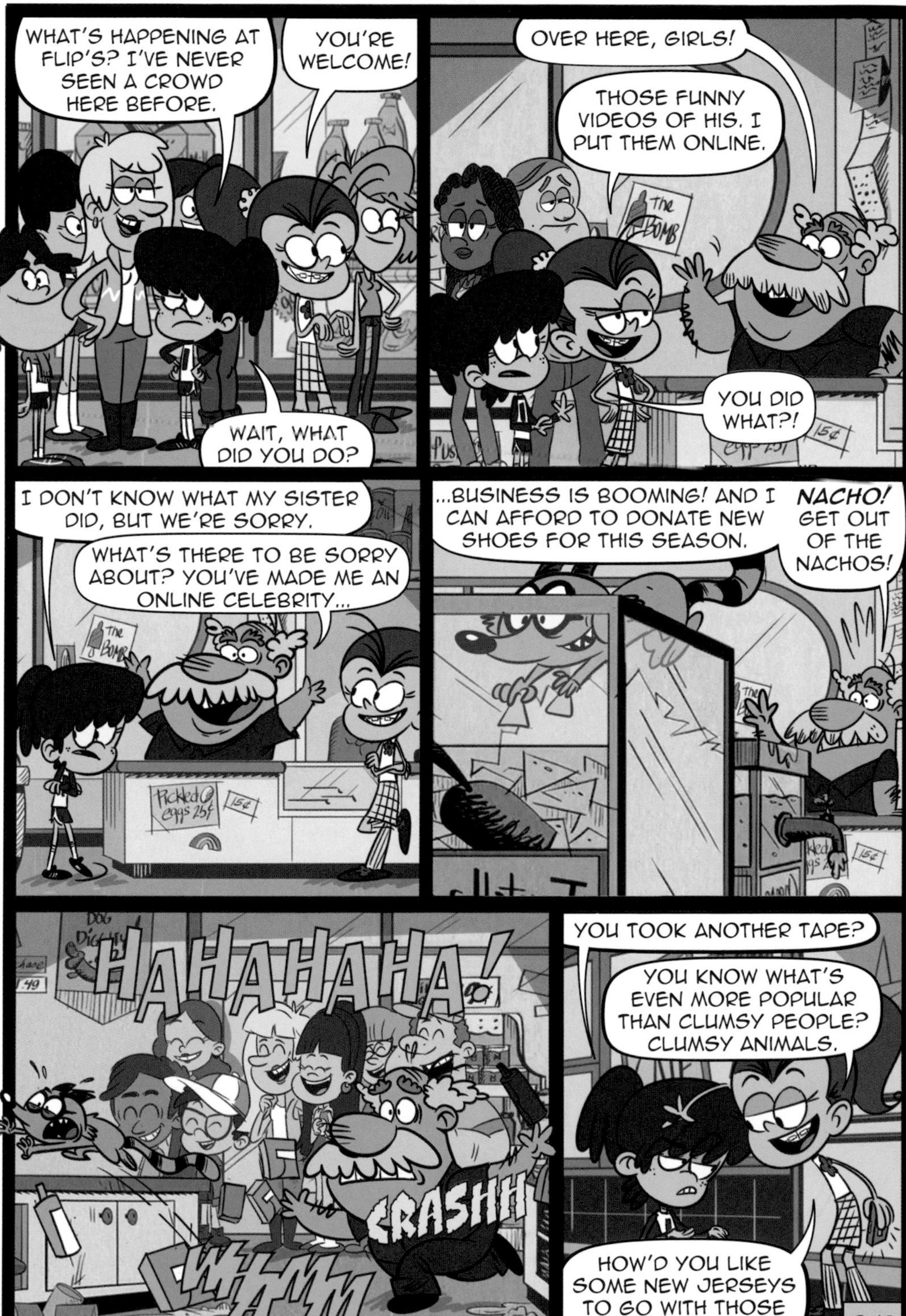
WHAT'S HAPPENING AT FLIP'S? I'VE NEVER SEEN A CROWD HERE BEFORE.
YOU'RE WELCOME!
WAIT, WHAT DID YOU DO?
OVER HERE, GIRLS!
THOSE FUNNY VIDEOS OF HIS. I PUT THEM ONLINE.
YOU DID WHAT?!
I DON'T KNOW WHAT MY SISTER DID, BUT WE'RE SORRY.
WHAT'S THERE TO BE SORRY ABOUT? YOU'VE MADE ME AN ONLINE CELEBRITY...
Pickled eggs 25¢
15¢
...BUSINESS IS BOOMING! AND I CAN AFFORD TO DONATE NEW SHOES FOR THIS SEASON.
NACHO! GET OUT OF THE NACHOS!
HAHAHAHA!
CRASHH
CWHAMM
YOU TOOK ANOTHER TAPE?
YOU KNOW WHAT'S EVEN MORE POPULAR THAN CLUMSY PEOPLE? CLUMSY ANIMALS.
HOW'D YOU LIKE SOME NEW JERSEYS TO GO WITH THOSE NEW SHOES?
END

"STRIPES"

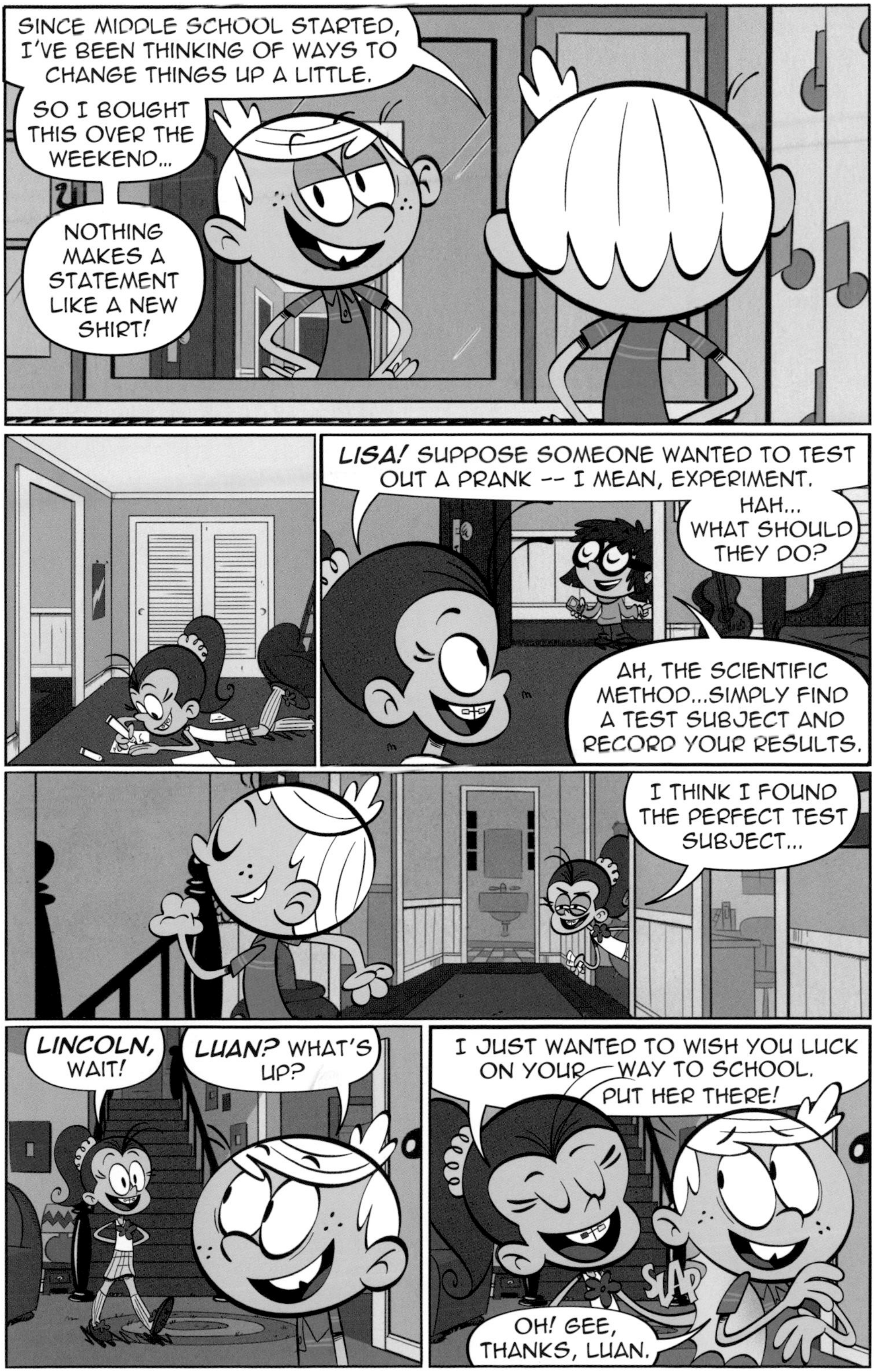
SINCE MIDDLE SCHOOL STARTED, I'VE BEEN THINKING OF WAYS TO CHANGE THINGS UP A LITTLE.
SO I BOUGHT THIS OVER THE WEEKEND...
NOTHING MAKES A STATEMENT LIKE A NEW SHIRT!
LISA! SUPPOSE SOMEONE WANTED TO TEST OUT A PRANK -- I MEAN, EXPERIMENT.
HAH... WHAT SHOULD THEY DO?
AH, THE SCIENTIFIC METHOD...SIMPLY FIND A TEST SUBJECT AND RECORD YOUR RESULTS.
I THINK I FOUND THE PERFECT TEST SUBJECT...
LINCOLN, WAIT!
LUAN? WHAT'S UP?
I JUST WANTED TO WISH YOU LUCK ON YOUR WAY TO SCHOOL.
PUT HER THERE!
SLAP
OH! GEE, THANKS, LUAN.

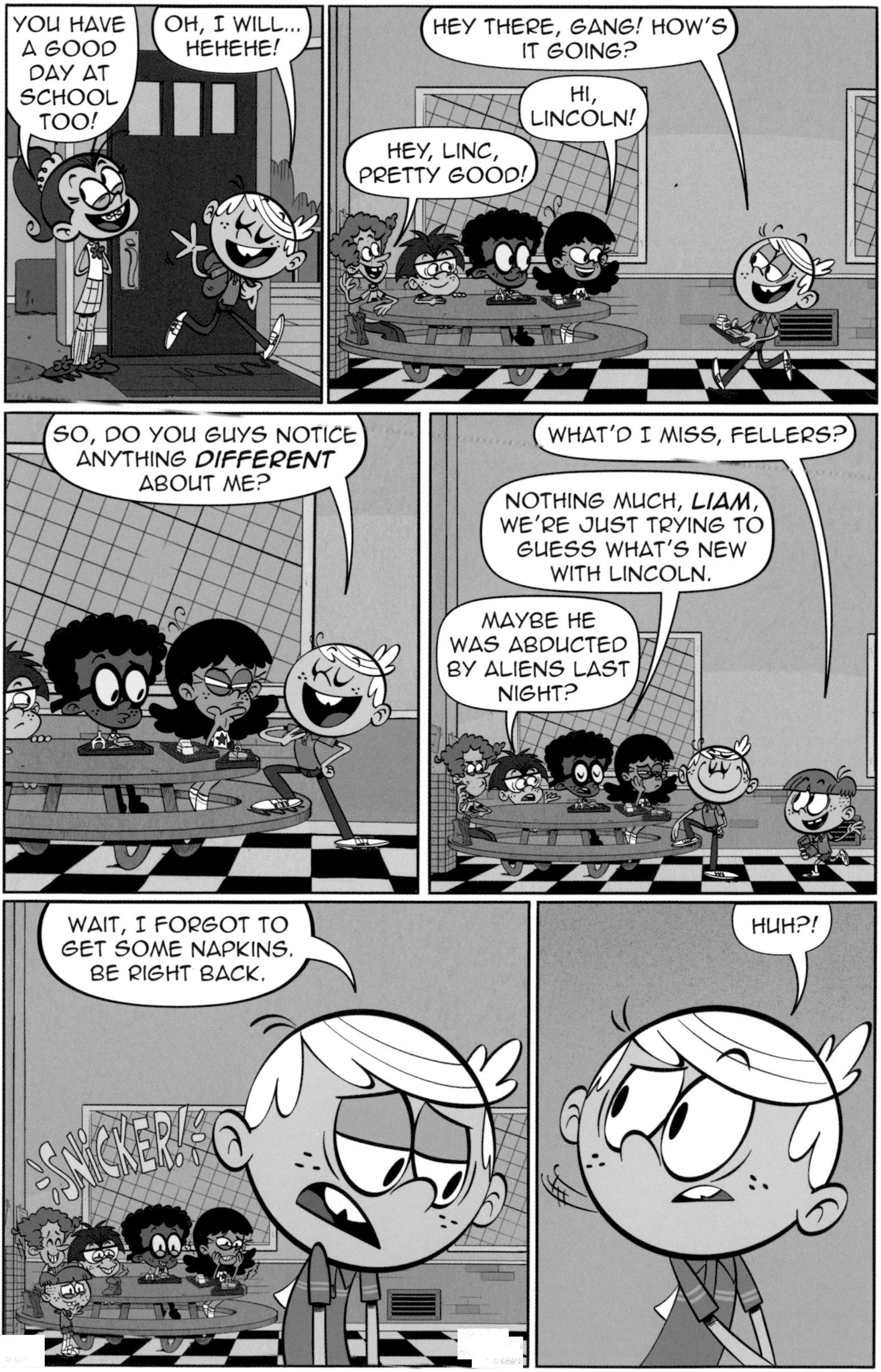
YOU HAVE A GOOD DAY AT SCHOOL TOO!
OH, I WILL... HEHEHE!
HEY THERE, GANG! HOW'S IT GOING?
HI, LINCOLN!
HEY, LINC, PRETTY GOOD!
SO, DO YOU GUYS NOTICE ANYTHING *DIFFERENT* ABOUT ME?
WHAT'D I MISS, FELLERS?
NOTHING MUCH, *LIAM*, WE'RE JUST TRYING TO GUESS WHAT'S NEW WITH LINCOLN.
MAYBE HE WAS ABDUCTED BY ALIENS LAST NIGHT?
WAIT, I FORGOT TO GET SOME NAPKINS. BE RIGHT BACK.
SNICKER!
HUH?!

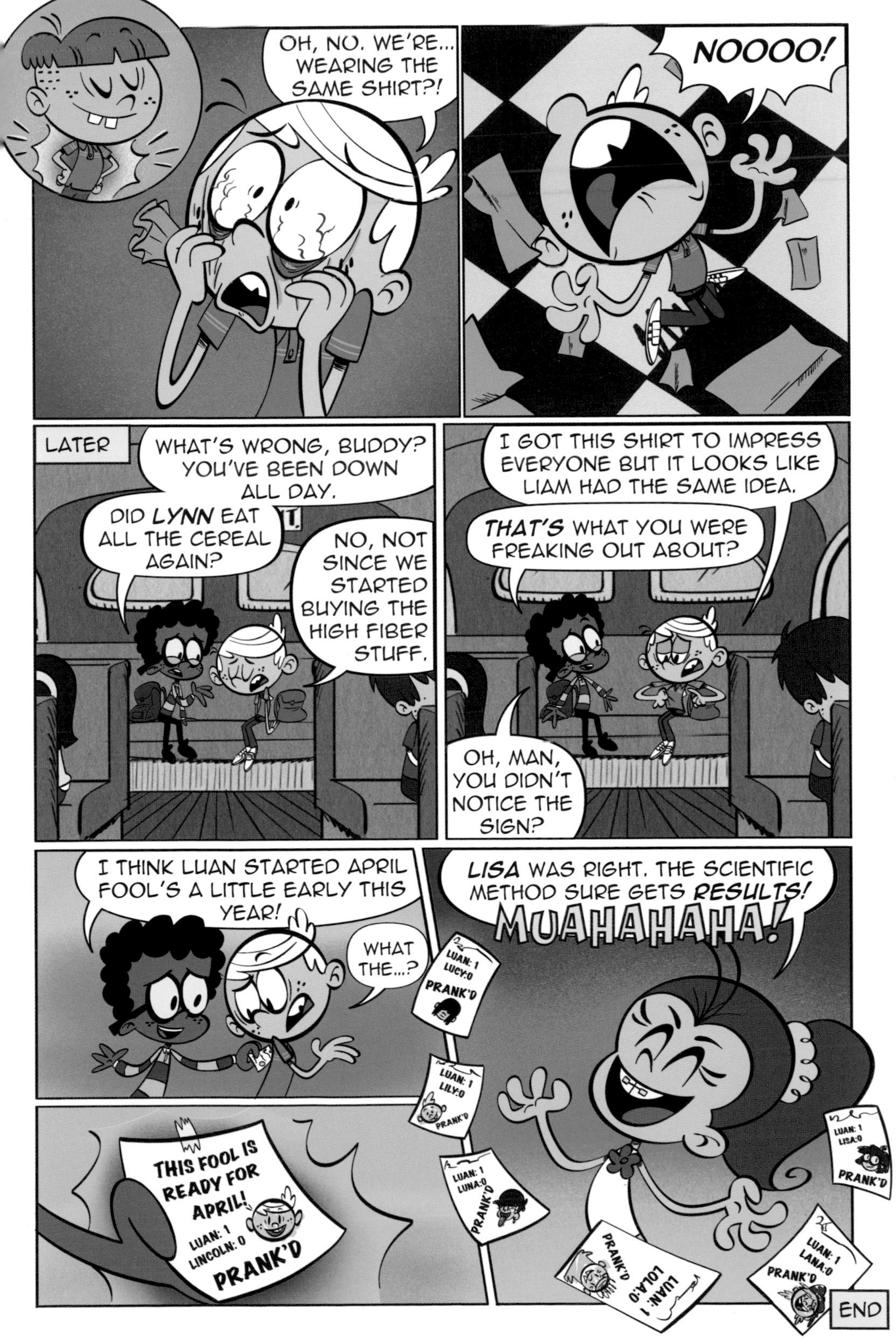
OH, NO. WE'RE... WEARING THE SAME SHIRT?!
NOOOO!
LATER
WHAT'S WRONG, BUDDY? YOU'VE BEEN DOWN ALL DAY.
DID LYNN EAT ALL THE CEREAL AGAIN?
NO, NOT SINCE WE STARTED BUYING THE HIGH FIBER STUFF.
I GOT THIS SHIRT TO IMPRESS EVERYONE BUT IT LOOKS LIKE LIAM HAD THE SAME IDEA.
THAT'S WHAT YOU WERE FREAKING OUT ABOUT?
OH, MAN, YOU DIDN'T NOTICE THE SIGN?
I THINK LUAN STARTED APRIL FOOL'S A LITTLE EARLY THIS YEAR!
WHAT THE...?
THIS FOOL IS READY FOR APRIL!
LUAN: 1
LINCOLN: 0
PRANK'D
LISA WAS RIGHT. THE SCIENTIFIC METHOD SURE GETS RESULTS!
MUAHAHAHA!
LUAN: 1
LUCY:0
PRANK'D
LUAN: 1
LILY:0
PRANK'D
LUAN: 1
LUNA:0
PRANK'D
LUAN: 1
LISA:0
PRANK'D
LUAN: 1
LOLA:0
PRANK'D
LUAN: 1
LANA:0
PRANK'D
END

"SKATE-OFF OF GLORY"

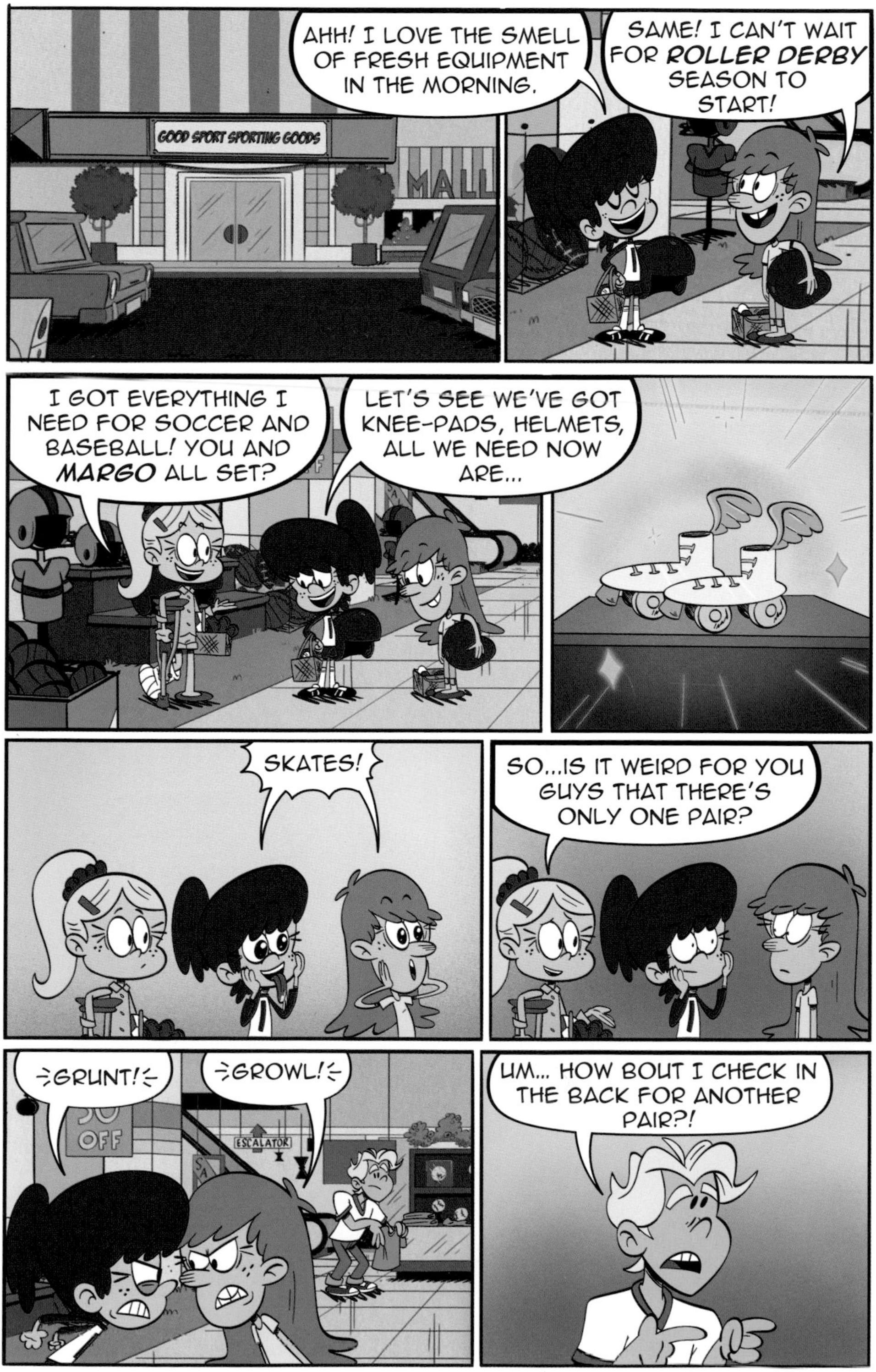
GOOD SPORT SPORTING GOODS
MALL
AHH! I LOVE THE SMELL OF FRESH EQUIPMENT IN THE MORNING.
SAME! I CAN'T WAIT FOR ROLLER DERBY SEASON TO START!
I GOT EVERYTHING I NEED FOR SOCCER AND BASEBALL! YOU AND MARGO ALL SET?
LET'S SEE WE'VE GOT KNEE-PADS, HELMETS, ALL WE NEED NOW ARE...
SKATES!
SO...IS IT WEIRD FOR YOU GUYS THAT THERE'S ONLY ONE PAIR?
GRUNT!
GROWL!
OFF
ESCALATOR
UM... HOW BOUT I CHECK IN THE BACK FOR ANOTHER PAIR?!

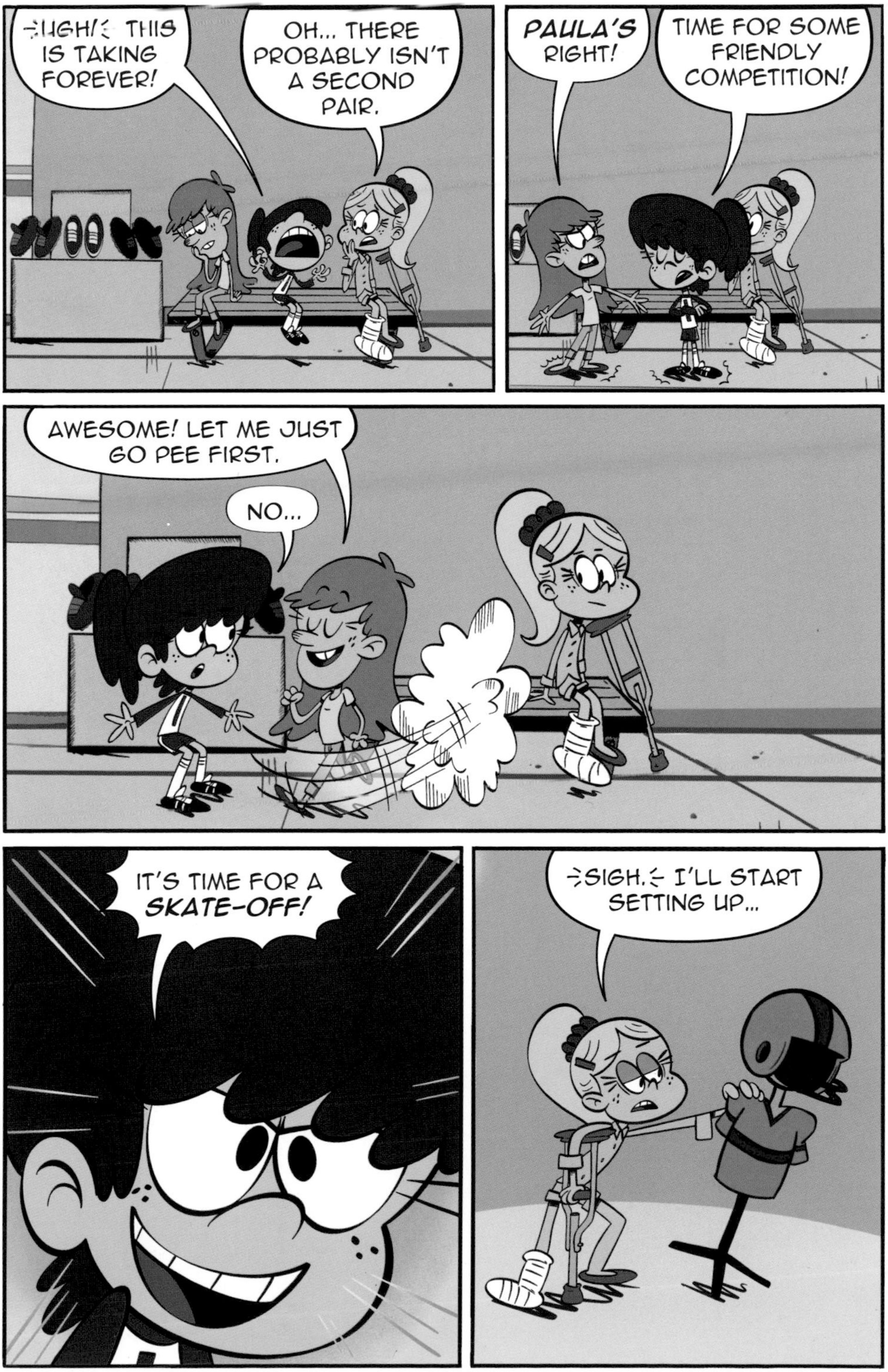

=UGH!= THIS IS TAKING FOREVER!
OH... THERE PROBABLY ISN'T A SECOND PAIR.
PAULA'S RIGHT!
TIME FOR SOME FRIENDLY COMPETITION!
AWESOME! LET ME JUST GO PEE FIRST.
NO...
IT'S TIME FOR A SKATE-OFF!
=SIGH.= I'LL START SETTING UP...

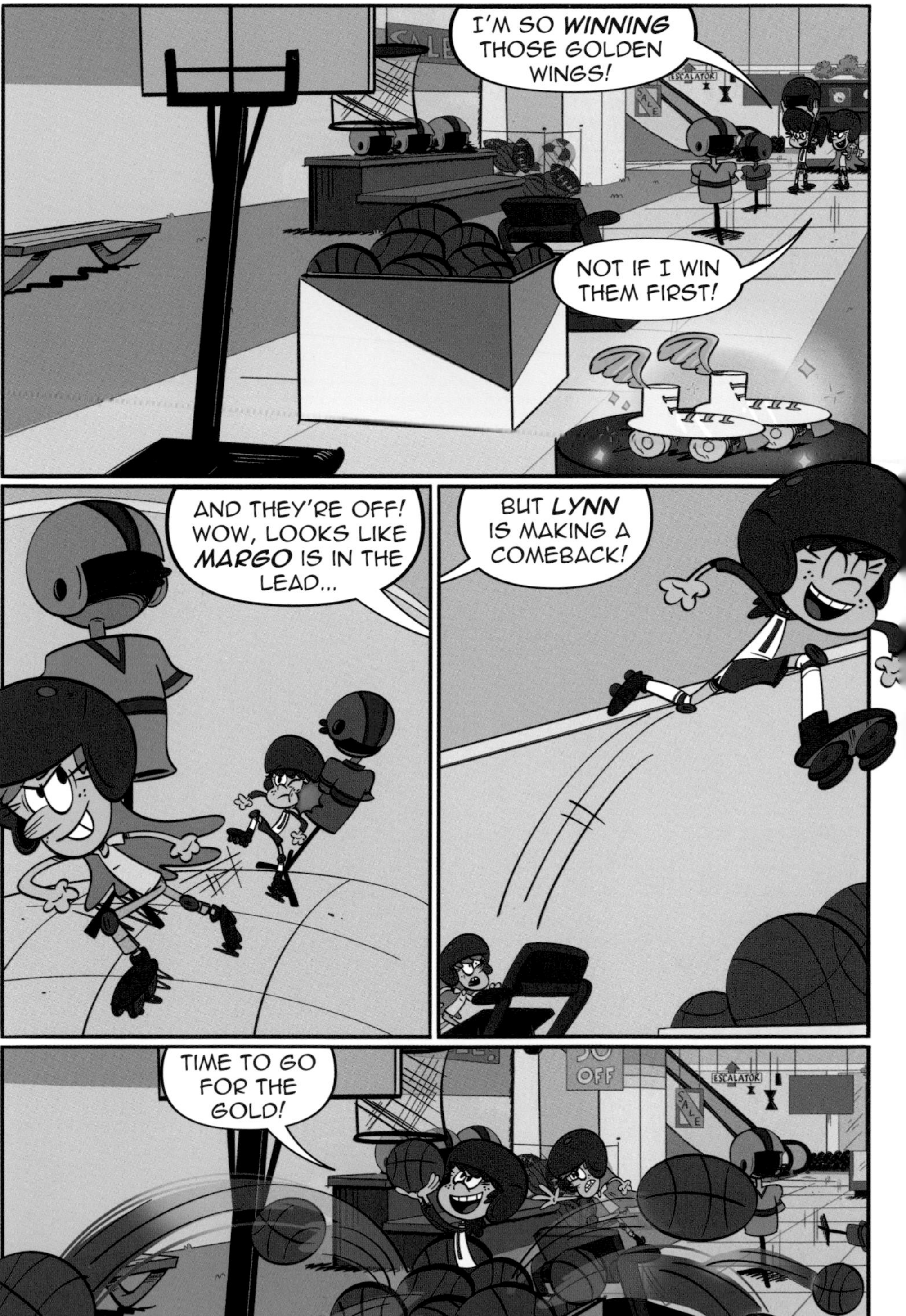
I'M SO WINNING THOSE GOLDEN WINGS!
NOT IF I WIN THEM FIRST!
AND THEY'RE OFF! WOW, LOOKS LIKE MARGO IS IN THE LEAD...
BUT LYNN IS MAKING A COMEBACK!
TIME TO GO FOR THE GOLD!

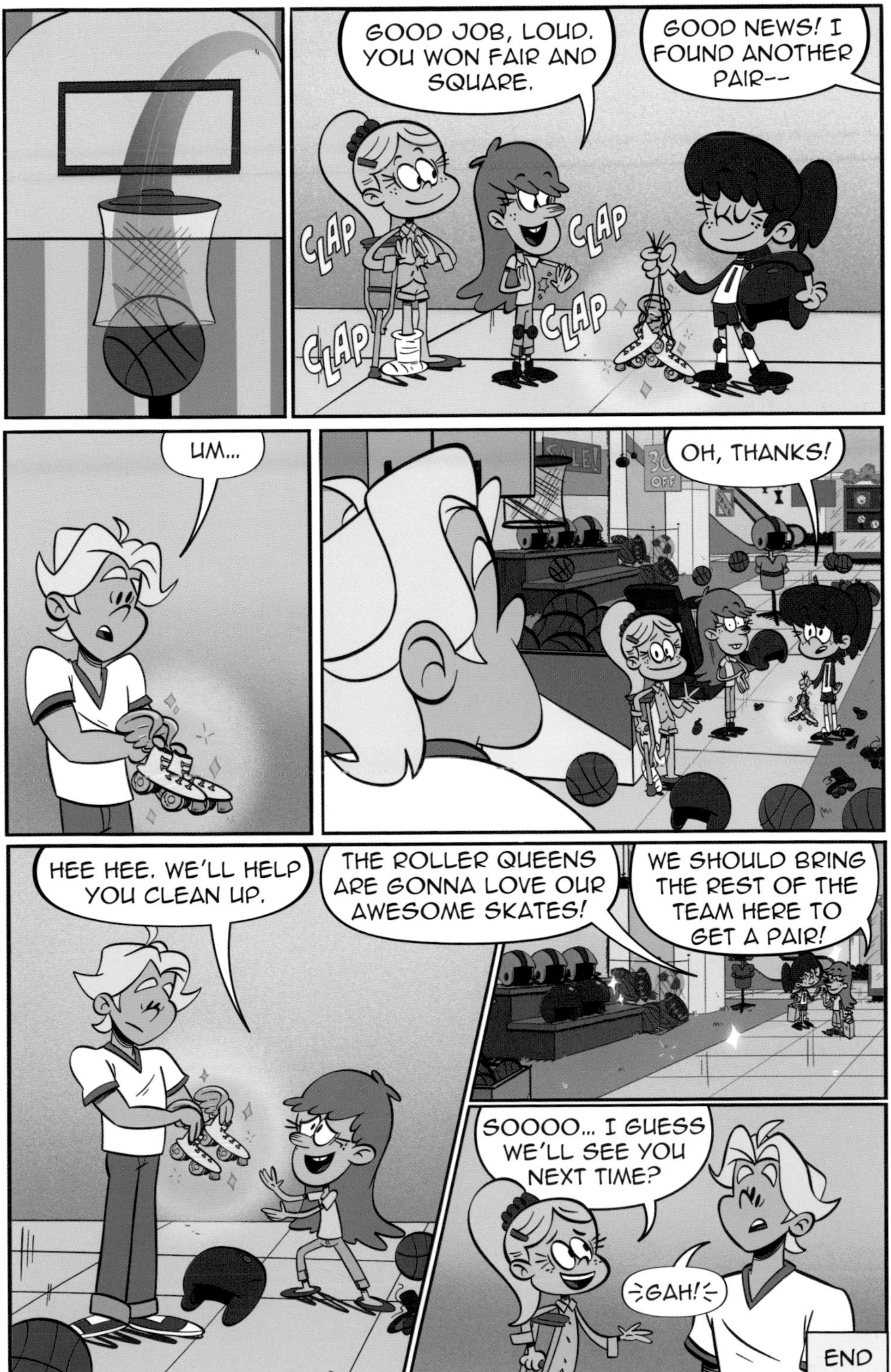
GOOD JOB, LOUD. YOU WON FAIR AND SQUARE.
GOOD NEWS! I FOUND ANOTHER PAIR--
CLAP
CLAP
CLAP
CLAP
UM...
OH, THANKS!
HEE HEE. WE'LL HELP YOU CLEAN UP.
THE ROLLER QUEENS ARE GONNA LOVE OUR AWESOME SKATES!
WE SHOULD BRING THE REST OF THE TEAM HERE TO GET A PAIR!
SOOOO... I GUESS WE'LL SEE YOU NEXT TIME?
GAH!
END

"STORY GAME BLAME"

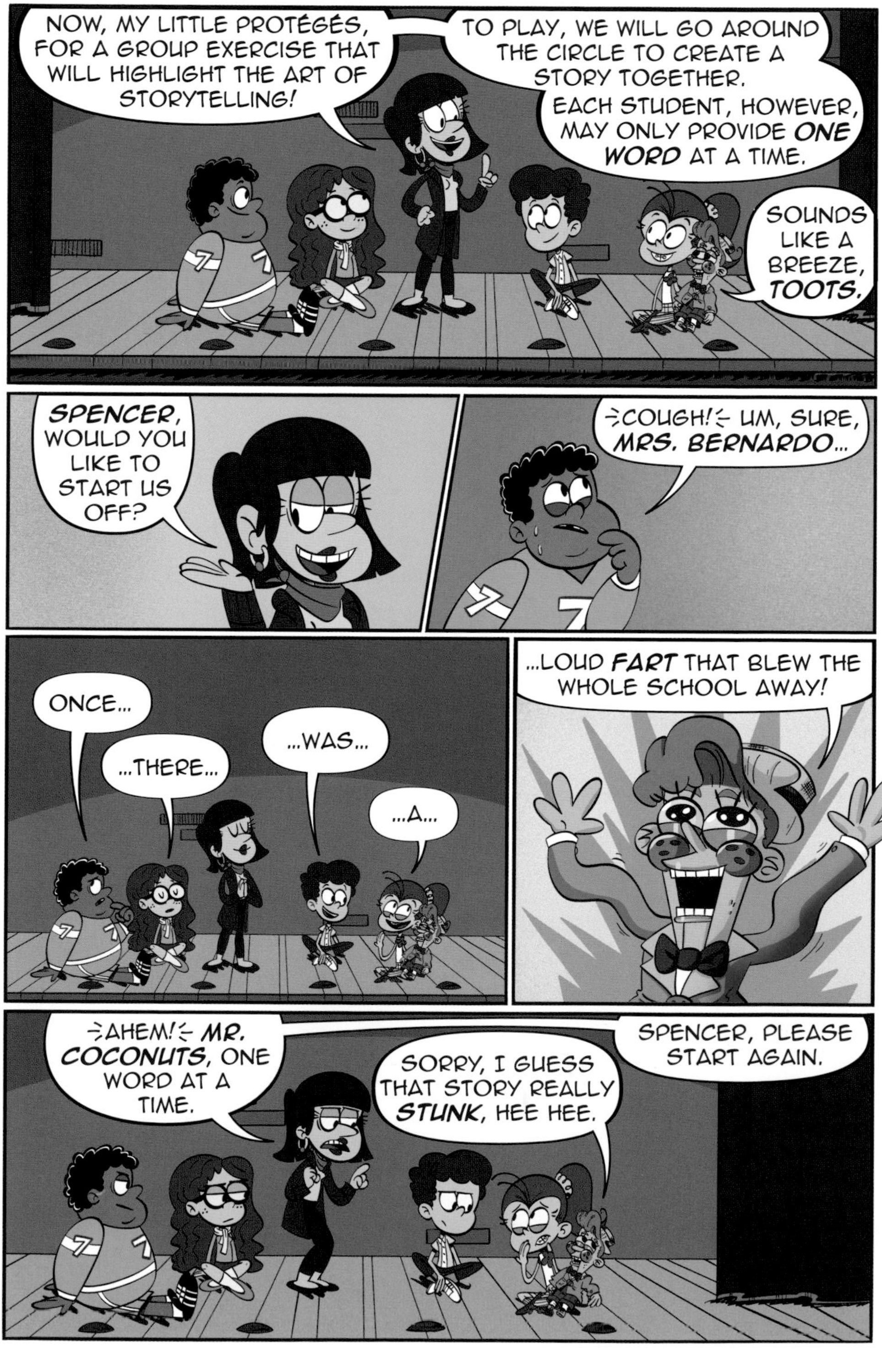

NOW, MY LITTLE PROTÉGÉS, FOR A GROUP EXERCISE THAT WILL HIGHLIGHT THE ART OF STORYTELLING!
TO PLAY, WE WILL GO AROUND THE CIRCLE TO CREATE A STORY TOGETHER.
EACH STUDENT, HOWEVER, MAY ONLY PROVIDE ONE WORD AT A TIME.
SOUNDS LIKE A BREEZE, TOTS.
SPENCER, WOULD YOU LIKE TO START US OFF?
COUGH! UM, SURE, MRS. BERNARDO...
ONCE...
...THERE...
...WAS...
...A...
...LOUD FART THAT BLEW THE WHOLE SCHOOL AWAY!
AHEM! MR. COCONUTS, ONE WORD AT A TIME.
SORRY, I GUESS THAT STORY REALLY STUNK, HEE HEE.
SPENCER, PLEASE START AGAIN.

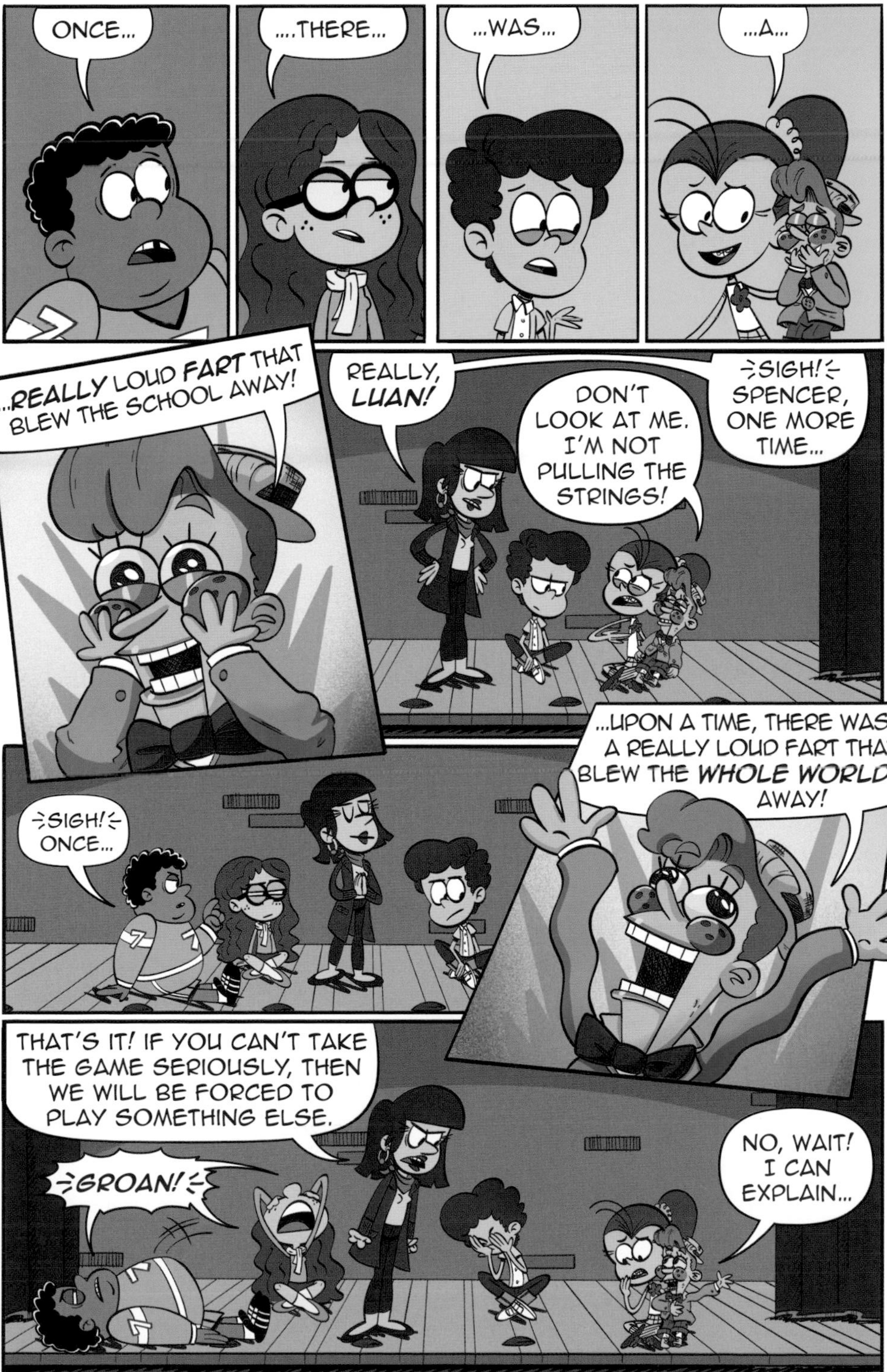
ONCE...
....THERE...
...WAS...
...A...
...REALLY LOUD FART THAT BLEW THE SCHOOL AWAY!
REALLY, LUAN!
DON'T LOOK AT ME. I'M NOT PULLING THE STRINGS!
SIGH! SPENCER, ONE MORE TIME...
SIGH! ONCE...
...UPON A TIME, THERE WAS A REALLY LOUD FART THAT BLEW THE WHOLE WORLD AWAY!
THAT'S IT! IF YOU CAN'T TAKE THE GAME SERIOUSLY, THEN WE WILL BE FORCED TO PLAY SOMETHING ELSE.
GROAN!
NO, WAIT! I CAN EXPLAIN...

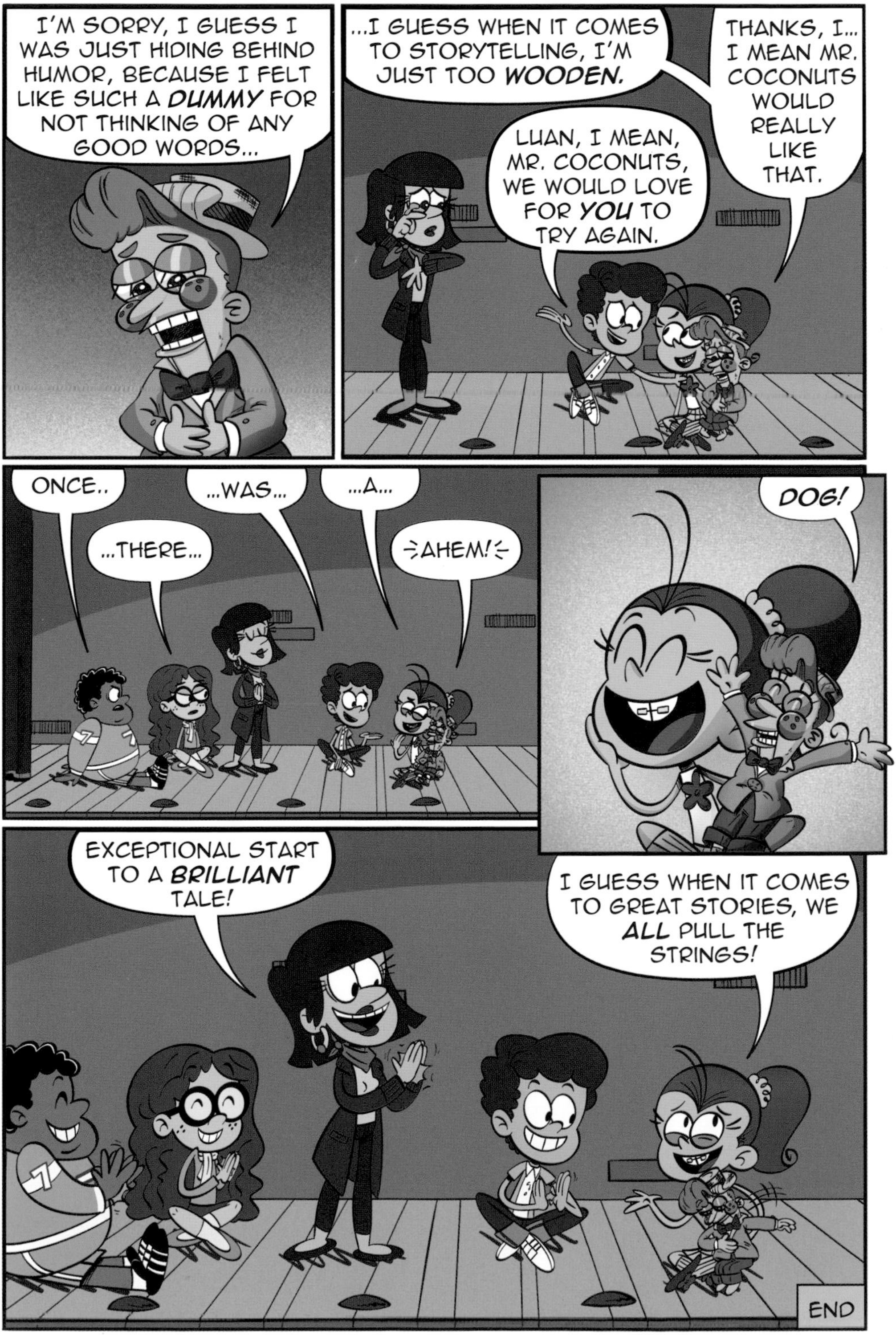
I'M SORRY, I GUESS I WAS JUST HIDING BEHIND HUMOR, BECAUSE I FELT LIKE SUCH A ***DUMMY*** FOR NOT THINKING OF ANY GOOD WORDS...
...I GUESS WHEN IT COMES TO STORYTELLING, I'M JUST TOO ***WOODEN.***
LUAN, I MEAN, MR. COCONUTS, WE WOULD LOVE FOR ***YOU*** TO TRY AGAIN.
THANKS, I... I MEAN MR. COCONUTS WOULD REALLY LIKE THAT.
ONCE..
...THERE...
...WAS...
...A...
AHEM!
DOG!
EXCEPTIONAL START TO A ***BRILLIANT*** TALE!
I GUESS WHEN IT COMES TO GREAT STORIES, WE ***ALL*** PULL THE STRINGS!
END

"UNIFORM UPHEAVAL"

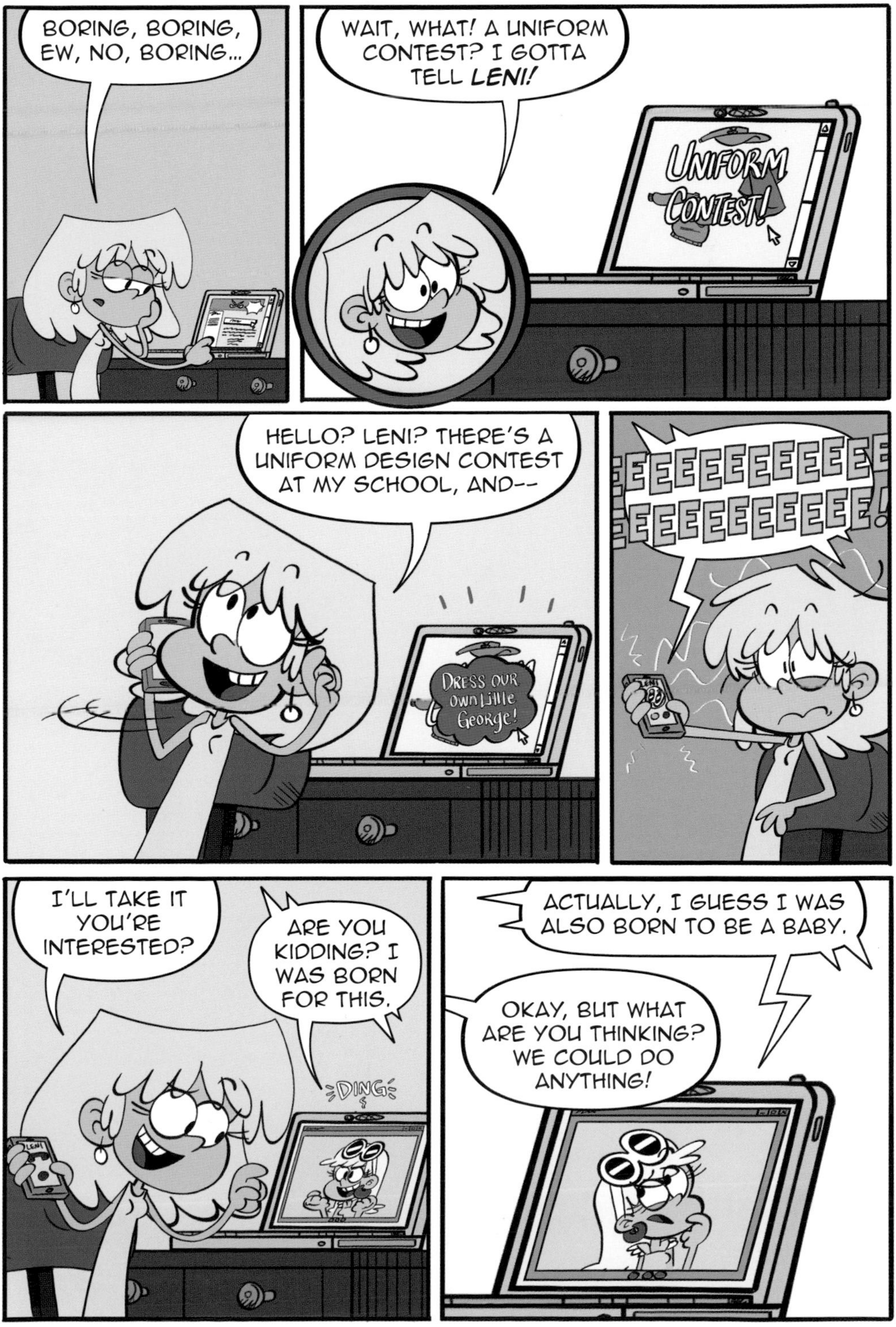
BORING, BORING, EW, NO, BORING...
WAIT, WHAT! A UNIFORM CONTEST? I GOTTA TELL LENI!
UNIFORM CONTEST!
HELLO? LENI? THERE'S A UNIFORM DESIGN CONTEST AT MY SCHOOL, AND--
Dress our own Little George!
EEEEEEEEEEEEEEEEEEEEEEEEE!
I'LL TAKE IT YOU'RE INTERESTED?
ARE YOU KIDDING? I WAS BORN FOR THIS.
DING
ACTUALLY, I GUESS I WAS ALSO BORN TO BE A BABY.
OKAY, BUT WHAT ARE YOU THINKING? WE COULD DO ANYTHING!

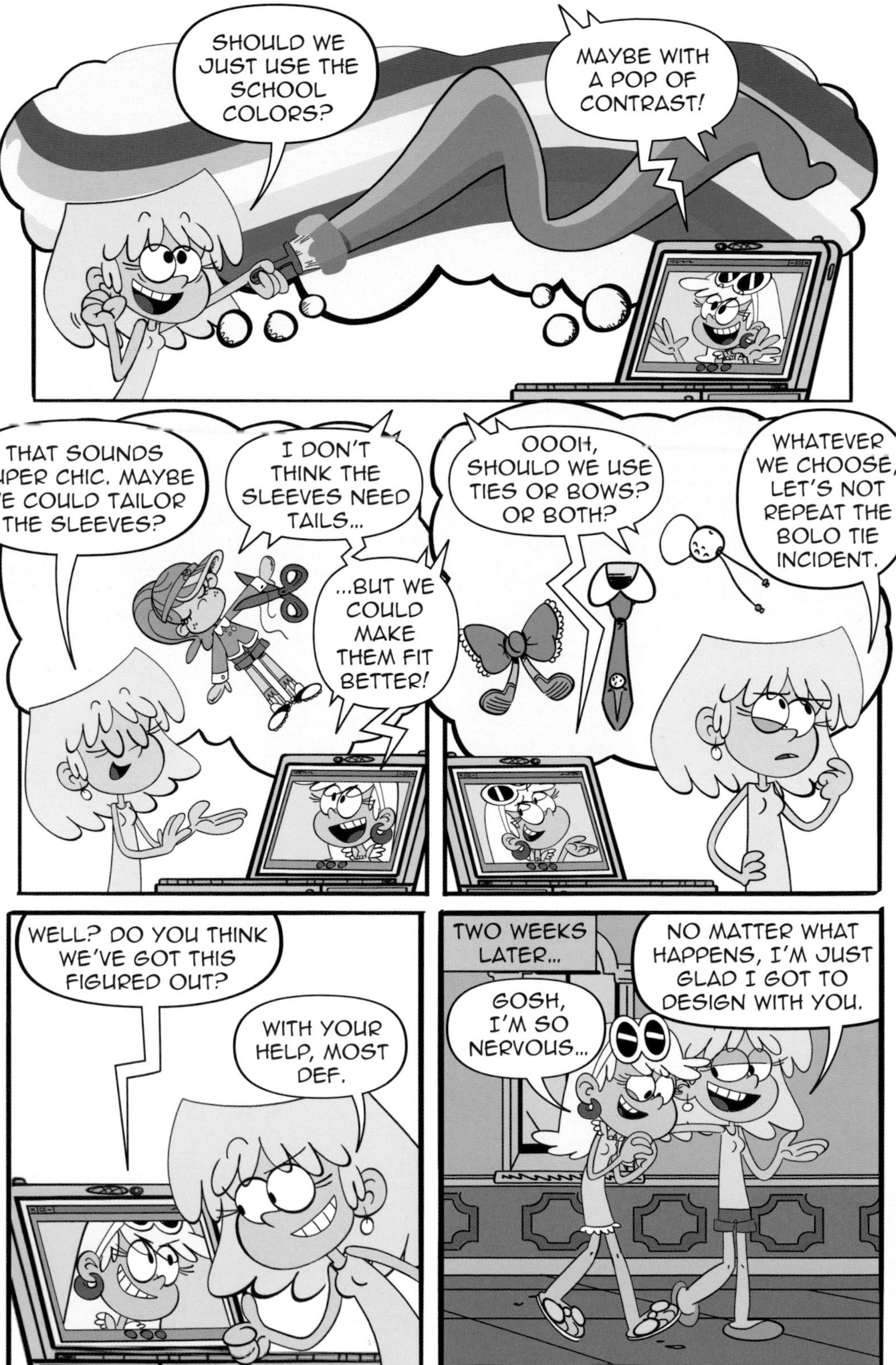
SHOULD WE JUST USE THE SCHOOL COLORS?
MAYBE WITH A POP OF CONTRAST!
THAT SOUNDS SUPER CHIC. MAYBE WE COULD TAILOR THE SLEEVES?
I DON'T THINK THE SLEEVES NEED TAILS...
...BUT WE COULD MAKE THEM FIT BETTER!
OOOH, SHOULD WE USE TIES OR BOWS? OR BOTH?
WHATEVER WE CHOOSE, LET'S NOT REPEAT THE BOLO TIE INCIDENT.
WELL? DO YOU THINK WE'VE GOT THIS FIGURED OUT?
WITH YOUR HELP, MOST DEF.
TWO WEEKS LATER...
GOSH, I'M SO NERVOUS...
NO MATTER WHAT HAPPENS, I'M JUST GLAD I GOT TO DESIGN WITH YOU.

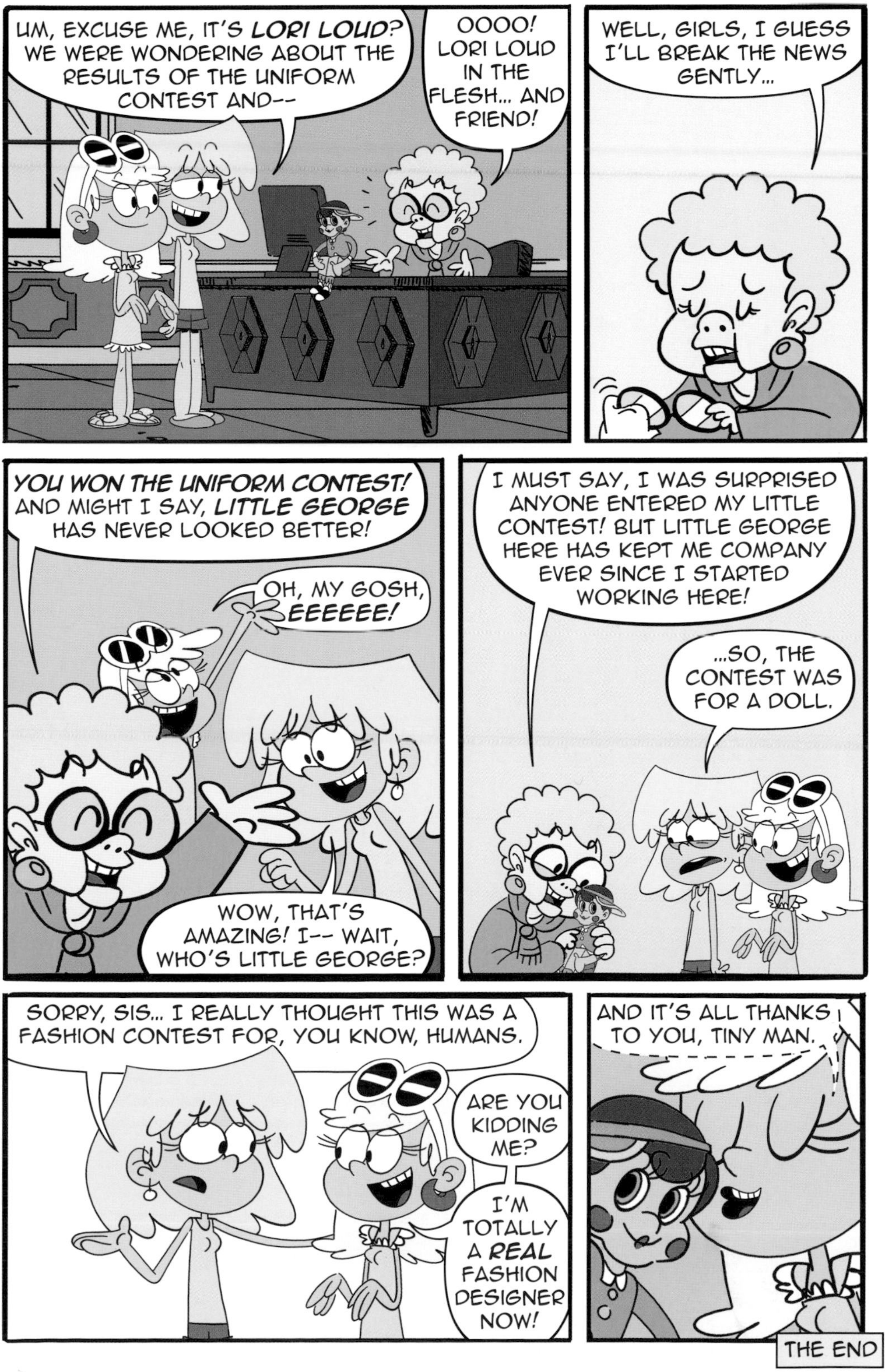

UM, EXCUSE ME, IT'S LORI LOUD? WE WERE WONDERING ABOUT THE RESULTS OF THE UNIFORM CONTEST AND--
OOOO! LORI LOUD IN THE FLESH... AND FRIEND!
WELL, GIRLS, I GUESS I'LL BREAK THE NEWS GENTLY...
YOU WON THE UNIFORM CONTEST! AND MIGHT I SAY, LITTLE GEORGE HAS NEVER LOOKED BETTER!
OH, MY GOSH, EEEEEE!
WOW, THAT'S AMAZING! I-- WAIT, WHO'S LITTLE GEORGE?
I MUST SAY, I WAS SURPRISED ANYONE ENTERED MY LITTLE CONTEST! BUT LITTLE GEORGE HERE HAS KEPT ME COMPANY EVER SINCE I STARTED WORKING HERE!
...SO, THE CONTEST WAS FOR A DOLL.
SORRY, SIS... I REALLY THOUGHT THIS WAS A FASHION CONTEST FOR, YOU KNOW, HUMANS.
ARE YOU KIDDING ME?
I'M TOTALLY A REAL FASHION DESIGNER NOW!
AND IT'S ALL THANKS TO YOU, TINY MAN.
THE END

“FLYER FACE-OFF”

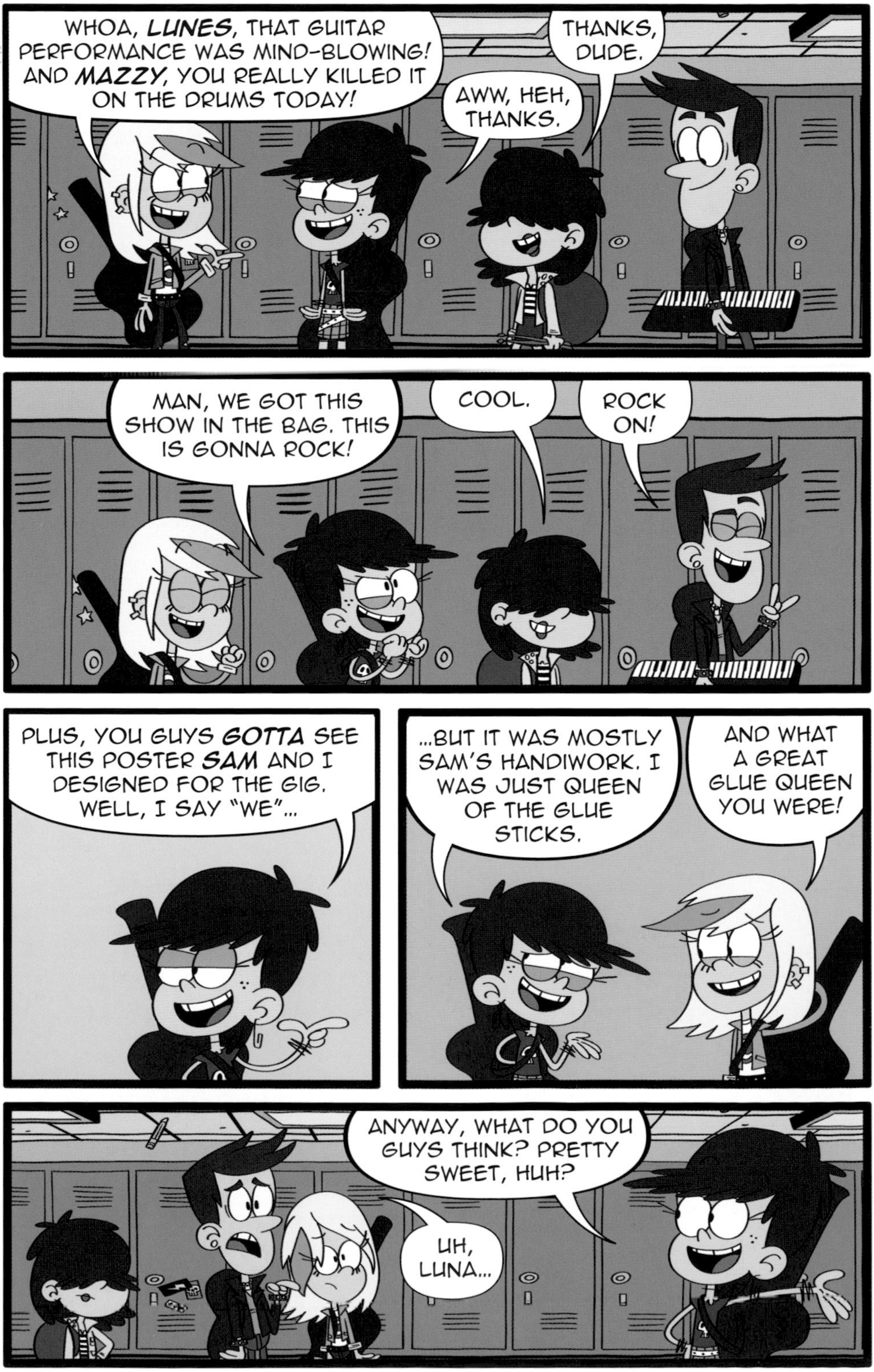

WHOA, *LUNES*, THAT GUITAR PERFORMANCE WAS MIND-BLOWING! AND *MAZZY*, YOU REALLY KILLED IT ON THE DRUMS TODAY!
AWW, HEH, THANKS.
THANKS, DUDE.
MAN, WE GOT THIS SHOW IN THE BAG. THIS IS GONNA ROCK!
COOL.
ROCK ON!
PLUS, YOU GUYS *GOTTA* SEE THIS POSTER *SAM* AND I DESIGNED FOR THE GIG. WELL, I SAY “WE”...
...BUT IT WAS MOSTLY SAM’S HANDIWORK. I WAS JUST QUEEN OF THE GLUE STICKS.
AND WHAT A GREAT GLUE QUEEN YOU WERE!
ANYWAY, WHAT DO YOU GUYS THINK? PRETTY SWEET, HUH?
UH, LUNA...

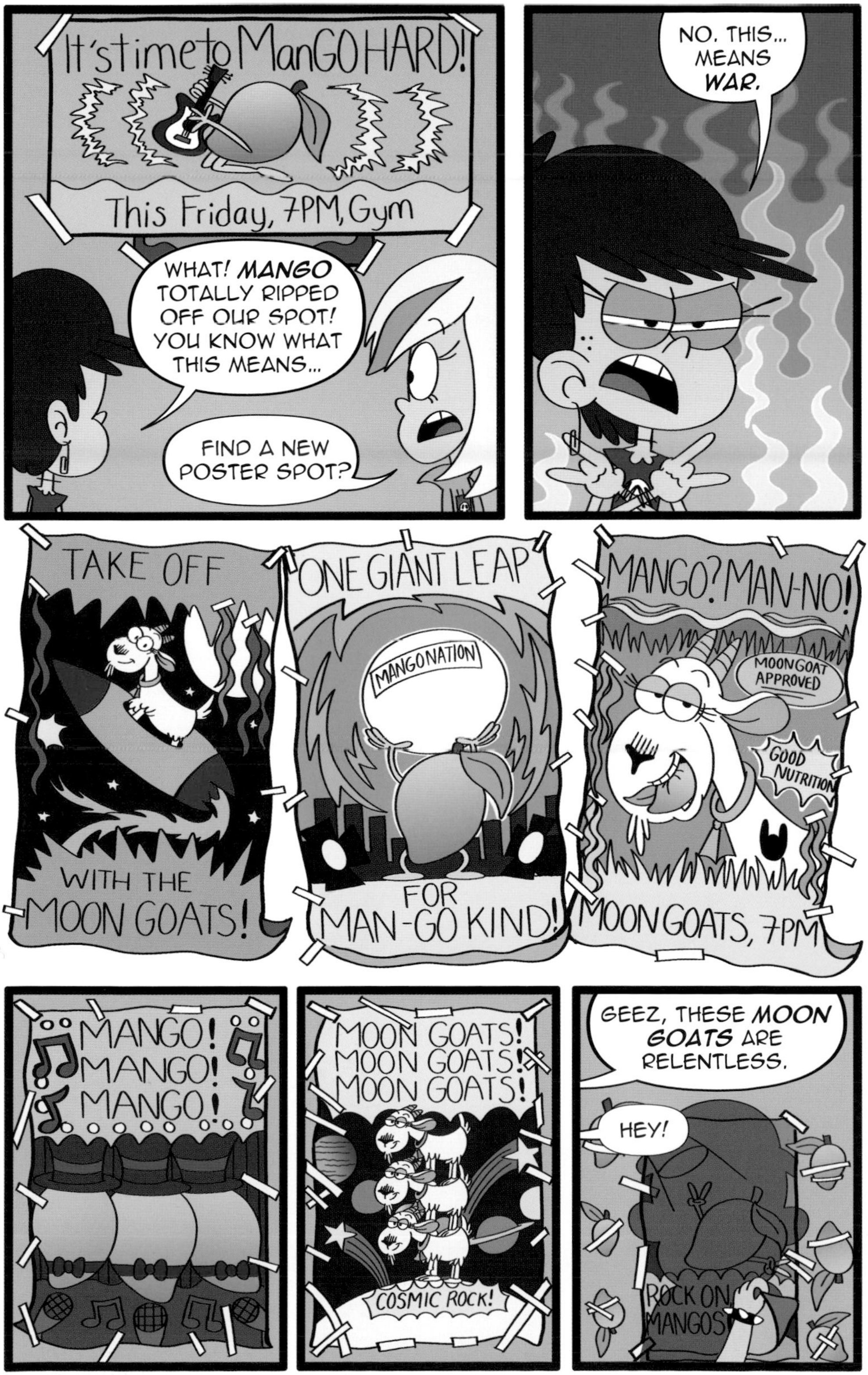
It's time to ManGO HARD!
This Friday, 7PM, Gym
WHAT! MANGO TOTALLY RIPPED OFF OUR SPOT! YOU KNOW WHAT THIS MEANS...
FIND A NEW POSTER SPOT?
NO. THIS... MEANS WAR.
TAKE OFF WITH THE MOON GOATS!
ONE GIANT LEAP FOR MAN-GO KIND!
MANGONATION
MANGO? MAN-NO!
MOONGOAT APPROVED
GOOD NUTRITION
MOON GOATS, 7PM
MANGO! MANGO! MANGO!
MOON GOATS! MOON GOATS! MOON GOATS!
COSMIC ROCK!
GEEZ, THESE MOON GOATS ARE RELENTLESS.
HEY!
ROCK ON MANGOS

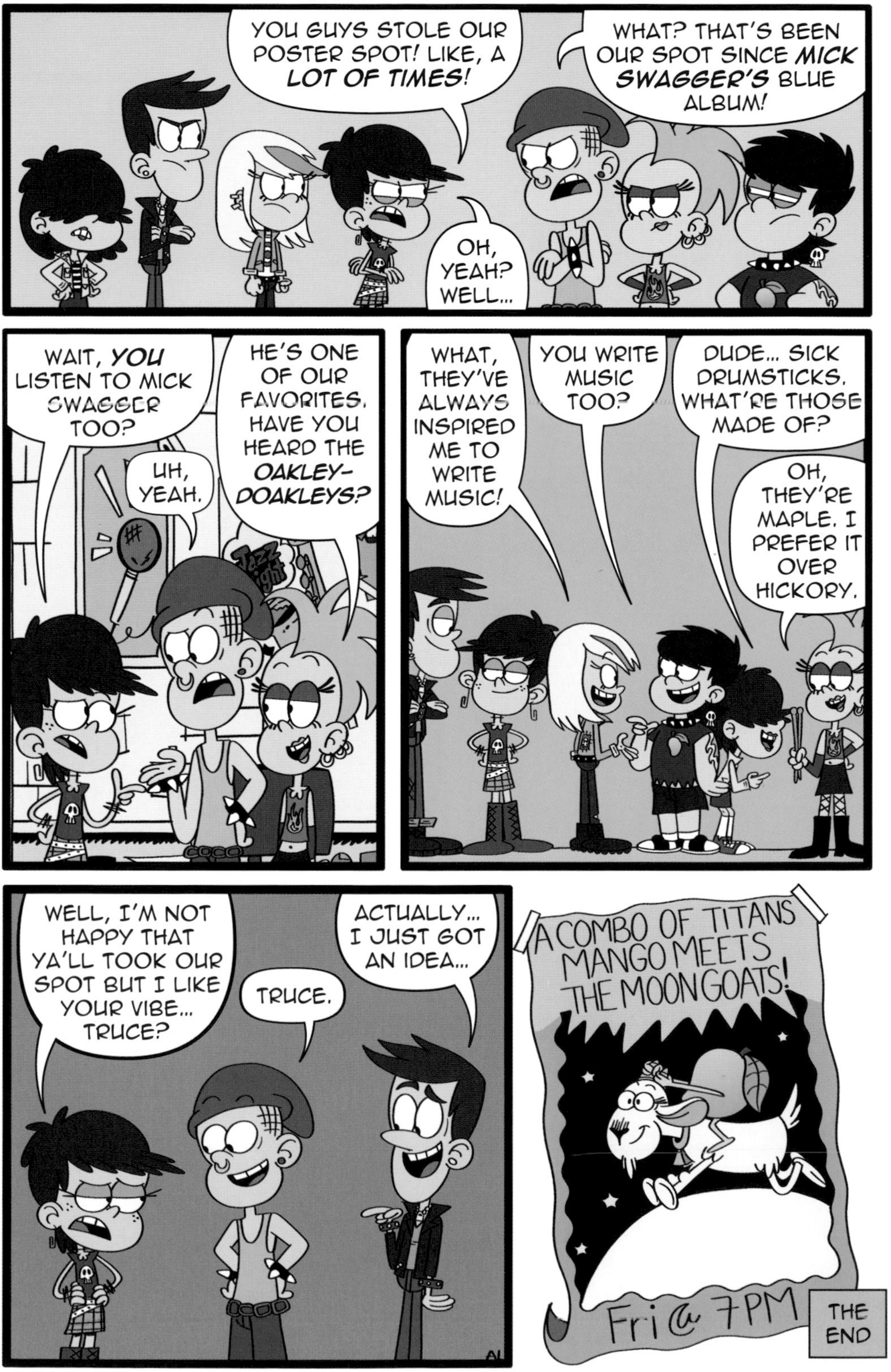
YOU GUYS STOLE OUR POSTER SPOT! LIKE, A LOT OF TIMES!
WHAT? THAT'S BEEN OUR SPOT SINCE MICK SWAGGER'S BLUE ALBUM!
OH, YEAH? WELL...
WAIT, YOU LISTEN TO MICK SWAGGER TOO?
UH, YEAH.
HE'S ONE OF OUR FAVORITES. HAVE YOU HEARD THE OAKLEY-DOAKLEYS?
WHAT, THEY'VE ALWAYS INSPIRED ME TO WRITE MUSIC!
YOU WRITE MUSIC TOO?
DUDE... SICK DRUMSTICKS. WHAT'RE THOSE MADE OF?
OH, THEY'RE MAPLE. I PREFER IT OVER HICKORY.
WELL, I'M NOT HAPPY THAT YA'LL TOOK OUR SPOT BUT I LIKE YOUR VIBE... TRUCE?
TRUCE.
ACTUALLY... I JUST GOT AN IDEA...
A COMBO OF TITANS
MANGO MEETS THE MOONGOATS!
Fri @ 7PM
THE END

"A BIG, BIG WORLD"

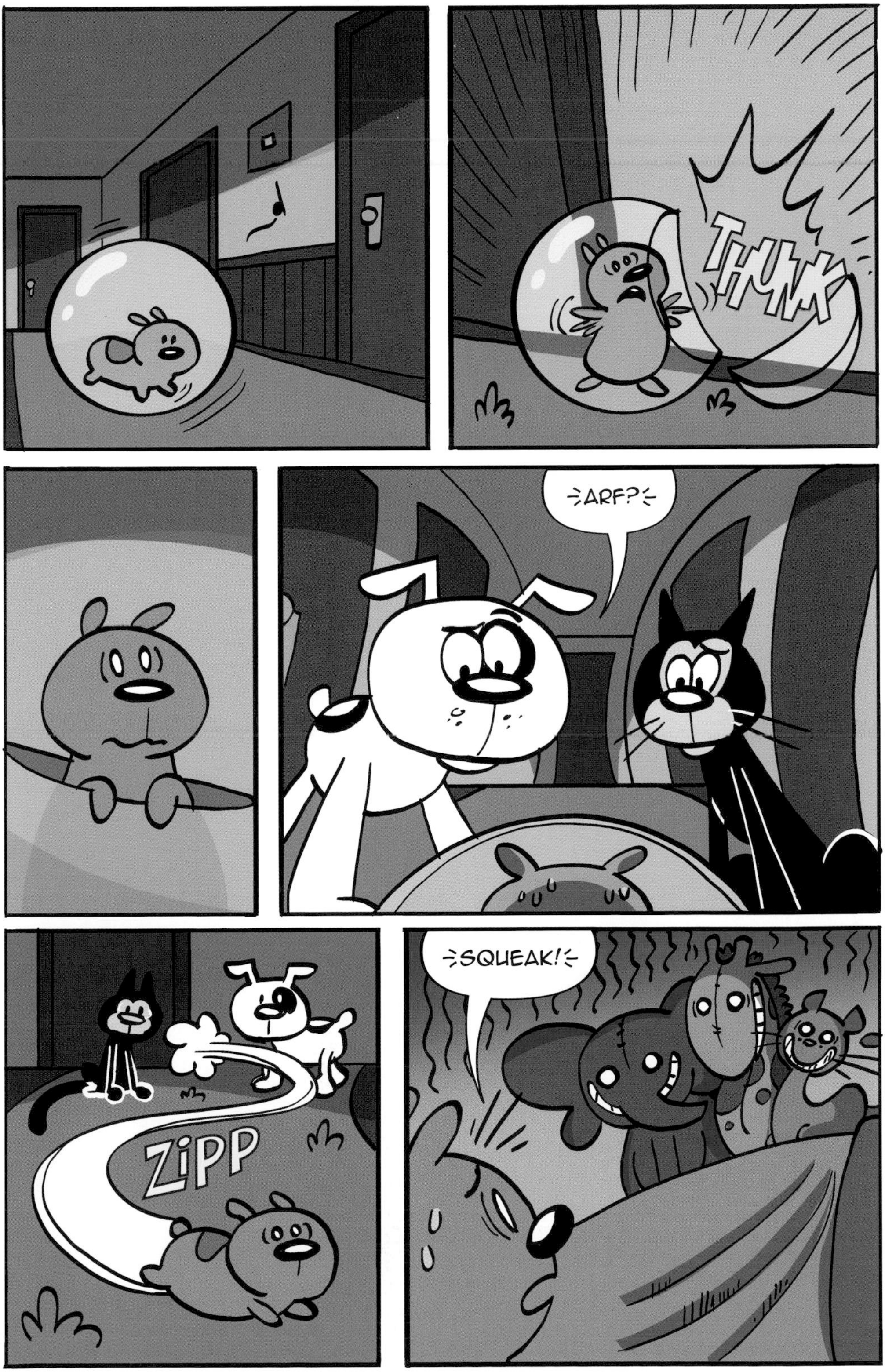
THUNK
ARF?
ZIPP
SQUEAK!

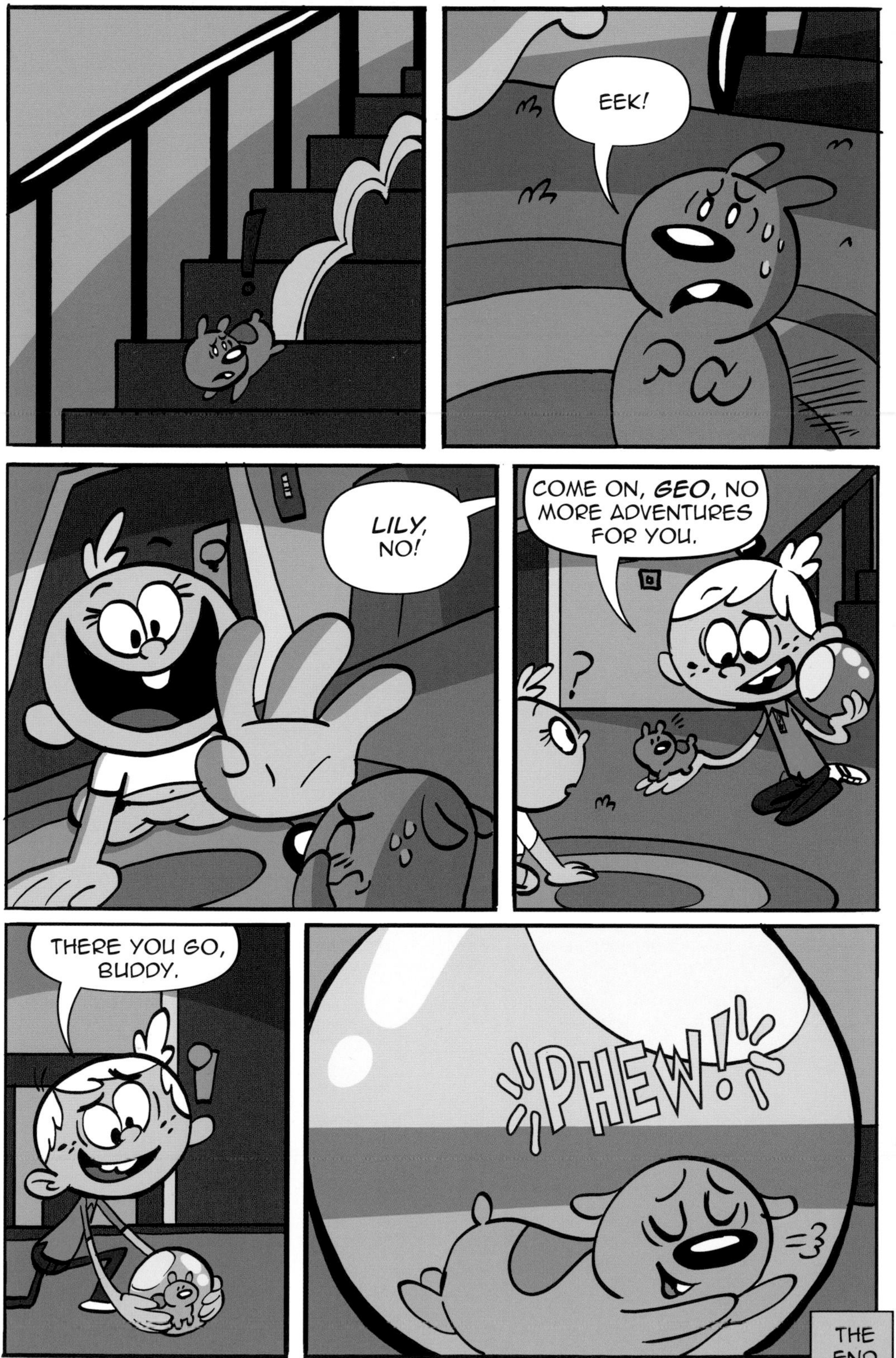

EEK!
LILY, NO!
COME ON, GEO, NO MORE ADVENTURES FOR YOU.
?
THERE YOU GO, BUDDY.
PHEW!
THE END

"LOUD OF THE THRONES"

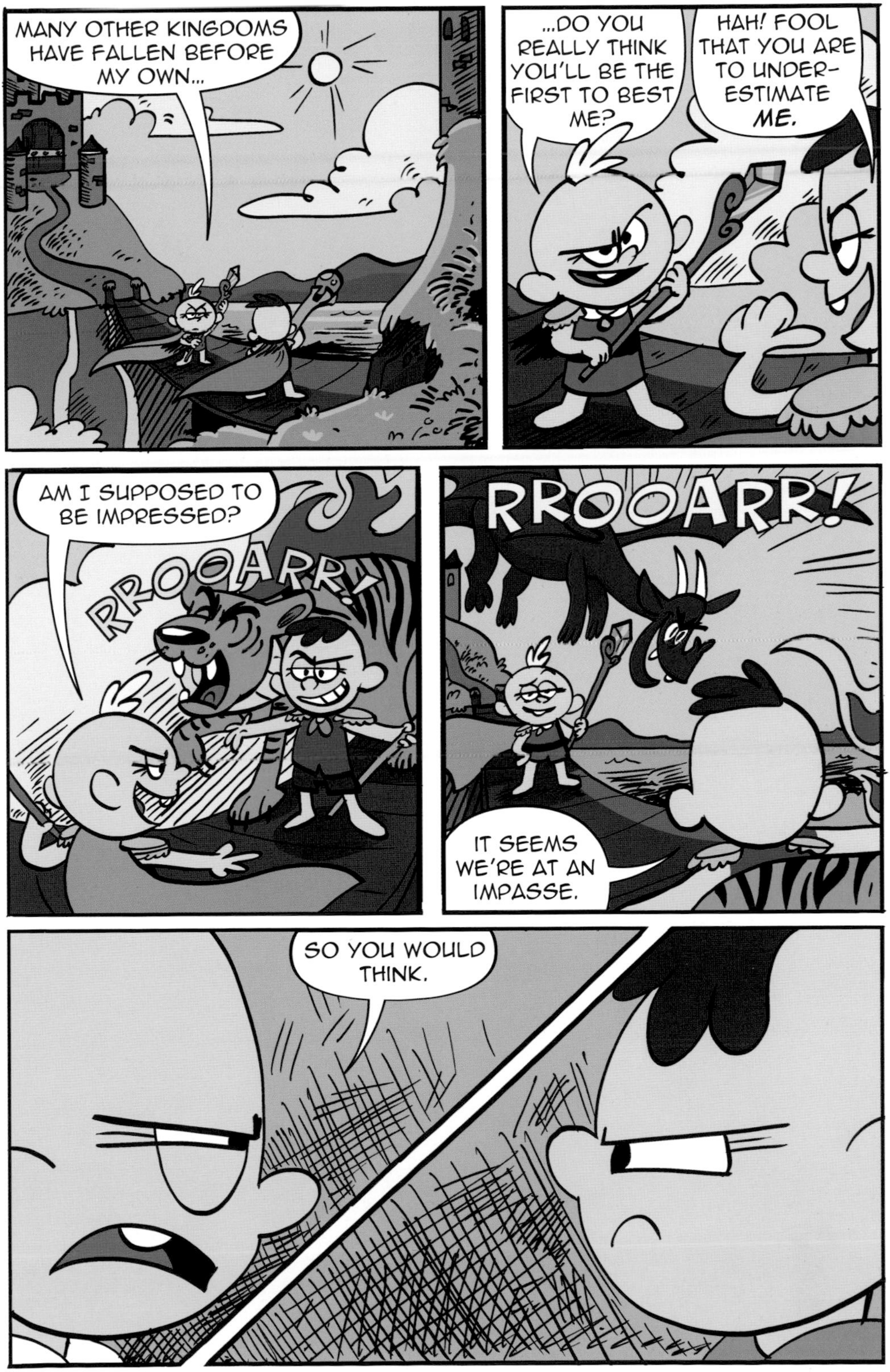
MANY OTHER KINGDOMS HAVE FALLEN BEFORE MY OWN...
...DO YOU REALLY THINK YOU'LL BE THE FIRST TO BEST ME?
HAH! FOOL THAT YOU ARE TO UNDER-ESTIMATE ME.
AM I SUPPOSED TO BE IMPRESSED?
RROOARR!
RROOARR!
IT SEEMS WE'RE AT AN IMPASSE.
SO YOU WOULD THINK.

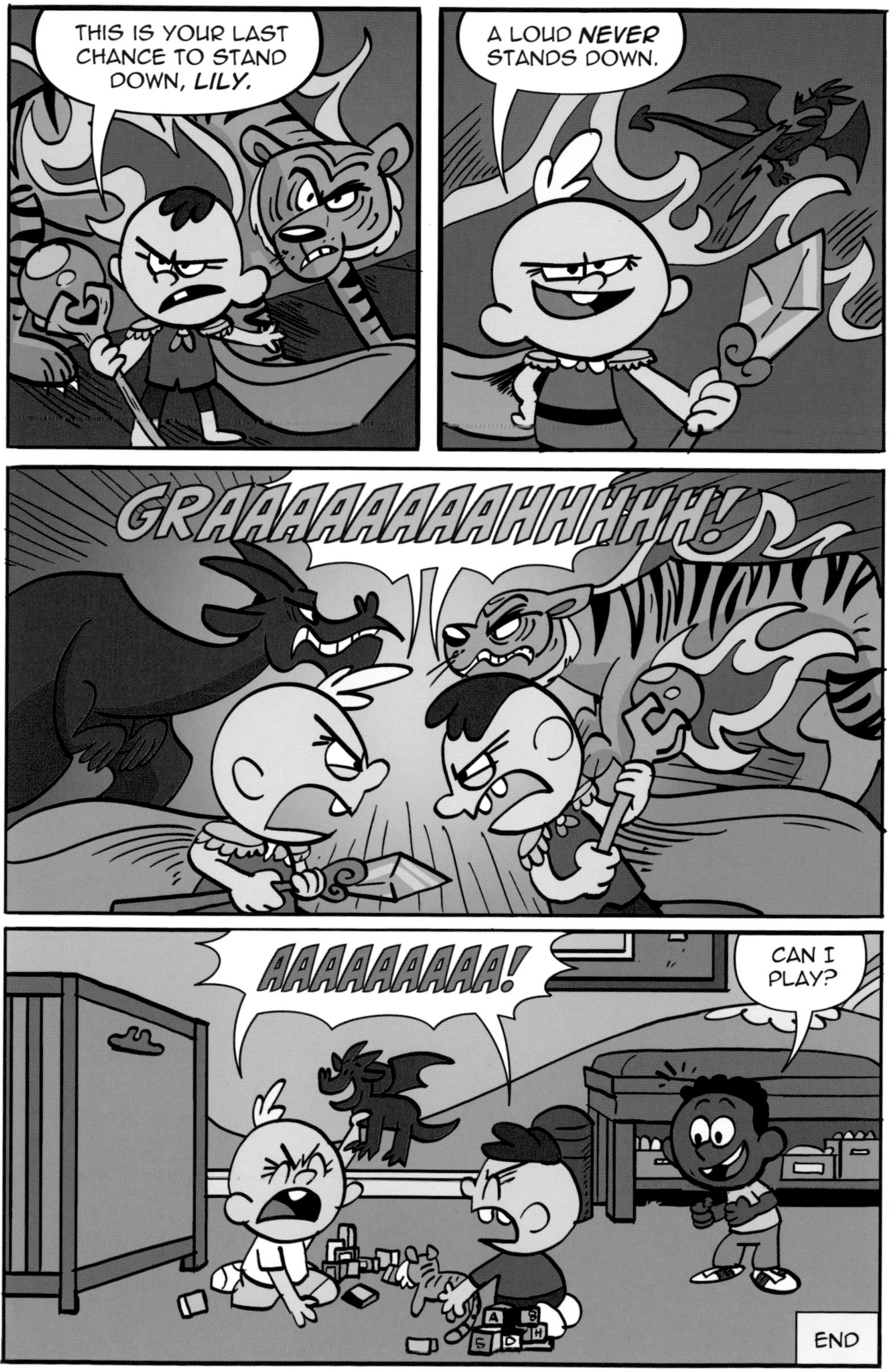
THIS IS YOUR LAST CHANCE TO STAND DOWN, LILY.
A LOUD NEVER STANDS DOWN.
GRAAAAAAAAAHHHHH!
AAAAAAAAA!
CAN I PLAY?
END

"HIDE-AND-CHIC"

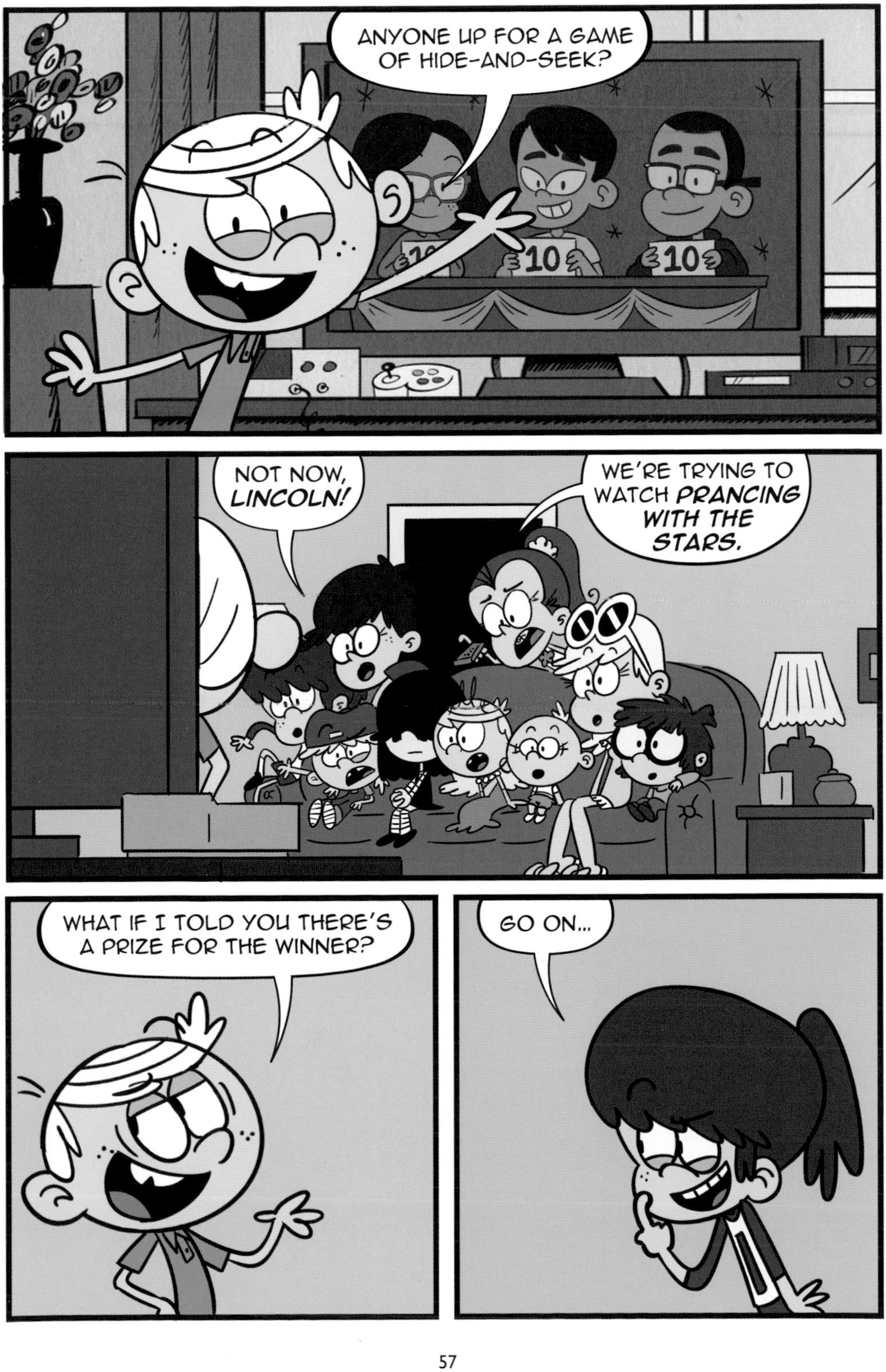
ANYONE UP FOR A GAME OF HIDE-AND-SEEK?
10
10
NOT NOW, ***LINCOLN!***
WE'RE TRYING TO WATCH ***PRANCING WITH THE STARS.***
WHAT IF I TOLD YOU THERE'S A PRIZE FOR THE WINNER?
GO ON...

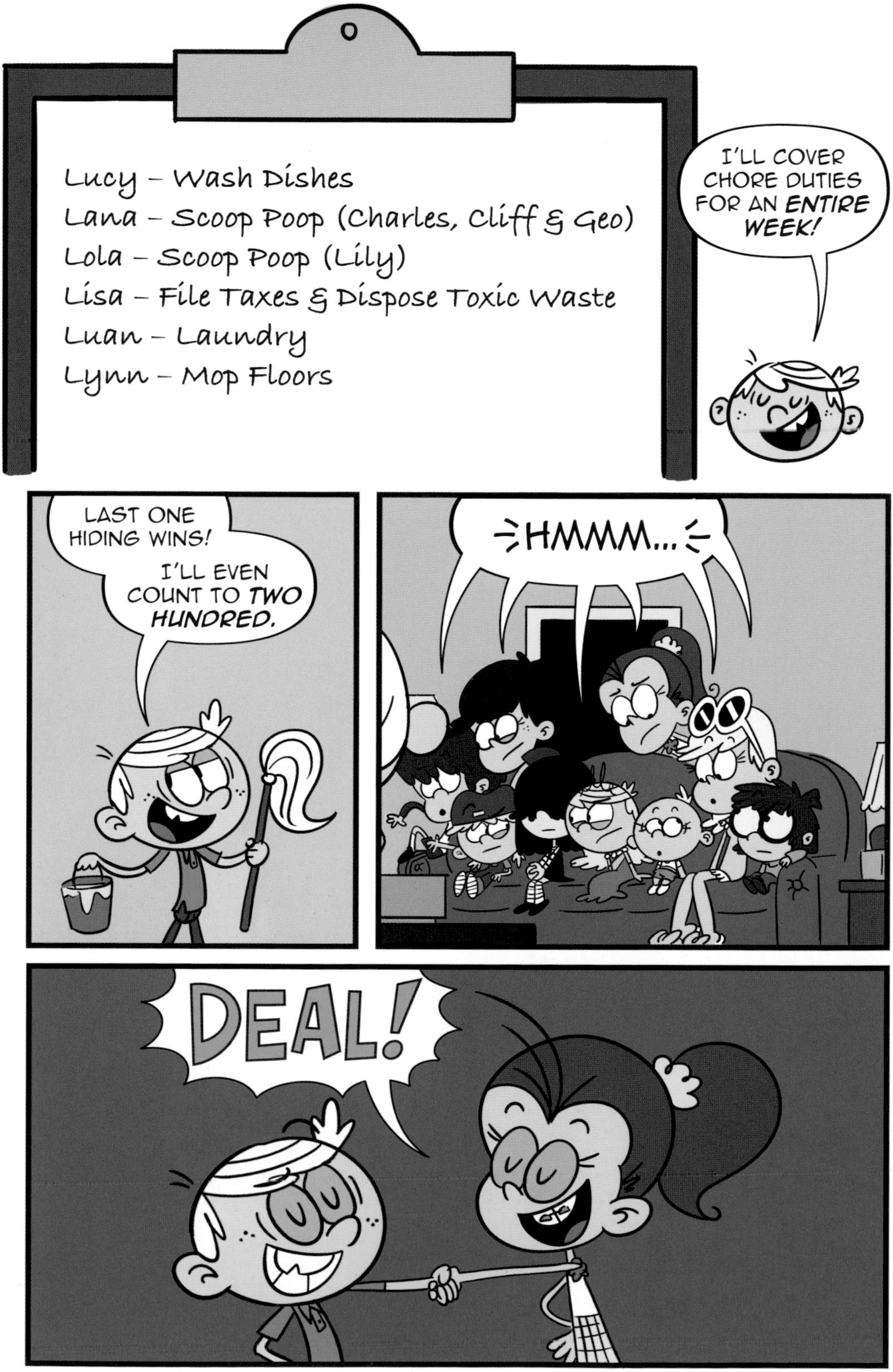
Lucy – Wash Dishes
Lana – Scoop Poop (Charles, Cliff & Geo)
Lola – Scoop Poop (Lily)
Lisa – File Taxes & Dispose Toxic Waste
Luan – Laundry
Lynn – Mop Floors
I'LL COVER CHORE DUTIES FOR AN *ENTIRE WEEK!*
LAST ONE HIDING WINS!
I'LL EVEN COUNT TO *TWO HUNDRED.*
HMMM...
DEAL!

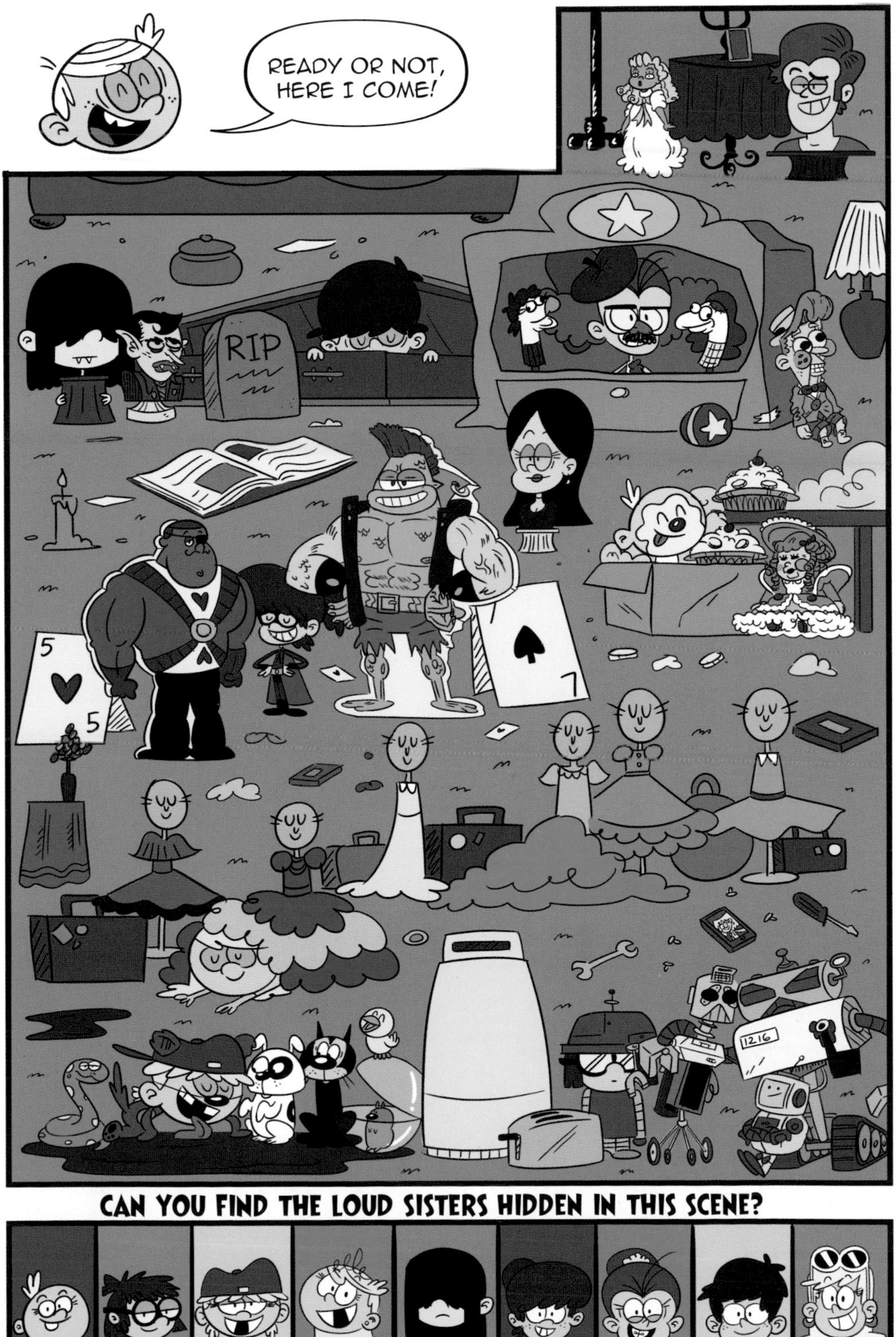
READY OR NOT, HERE I COME!
RIP
5
5
7
1216

CAN YOU FIND THE LOUD SISTERS HIDDEN IN THIS SCENE?

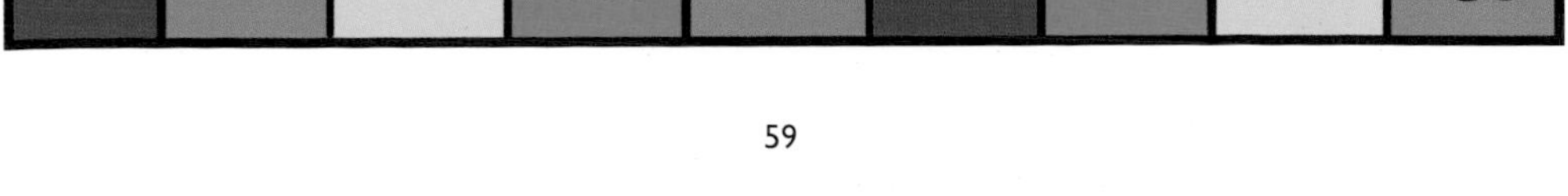

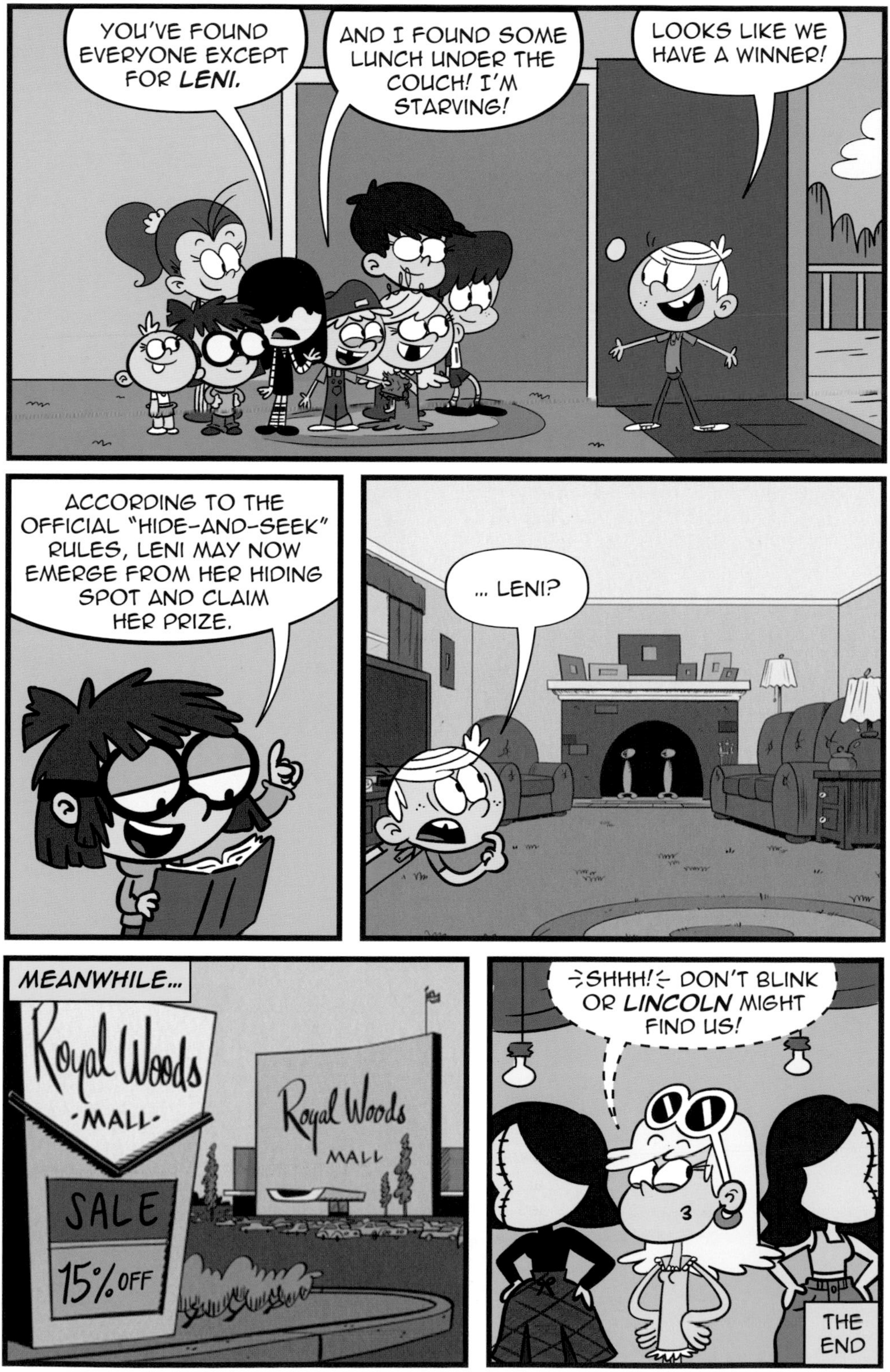
YOU'VE FOUND EVERYONE EXCEPT FOR LENI.
AND I FOUND SOME LUNCH UNDER THE COUCH! I'M STARVING!
LOOKS LIKE WE HAVE A WINNER!
ACCORDING TO THE OFFICIAL "HIDE-AND-SEEK" RULES, LENI MAY NOW EMERGE FROM HER HIDING SPOT AND CLAIM HER PRIZE.
... LENI?
MEANWHILE...
Royal Woods
·MALL·
SALE
15% OFF
Royal Woods
MALL
SHHH! DON'T BLINK OR LINCOLN MIGHT FIND US!
THE END

WATCH OUT FOR PAPERCUTZ™

Welcome to the stridently sonorous sixteenth volume of THE LOUD HOUSE, "Loud and Clear." As usual, it's from Papercutz, those perpetually palavering people dedicated to publishing great graphic novels for all ages. I'm Jim Salicrup, the Editor-in-Chief and Soft-talking Soul, here to get overly literal about the title of this graphic novel…

Unlike THE LOUD HOUSE show on Nickelodeon, the characters in THE LOUD HOUSE graphic novels neither move nor make any audible sounds. Comics, whether printed on paper or delivered digitally, are a silent medium (except for so-called "motion comics," which I think are really low-grade cartoons). Rather ironic that we're publishing a series with LOUD in the title, eh? In order for THE LOUD HOUSE comics to succeed, we need to have writers capture the way that Lincoln, his family and all his friends, speak on the show and have them "talk" the same way in the graphic novels. Fortunately, every story concept created for THE LOUD HOUSE graphic novels is looked over by the folks that produce the show to make sure everyone is in character. That way, if you're a fan of THE LOUD HOUSE on Nickelodeon, when you're reading THE LOUD HOUSE graphic novels, you "hear" the characters' voices in your head. (Also due to the magic of comics story-telling, your brain fills in the "movement" of the characters, as well.)

Let's go behind-the-scenes and meet the guy who truly makes sure that the dialogue and sound effects in every volume of THE LOUD HOUSE really are "Loud and Clear," allow me to introduce you to Wilson Ramos Jr, the letterer of almost every story in THE LOUD HOUSE graphic novels…

Wilson Ramos Jr. is a freelance comic artist who has worked in the comic industry for over 25 years. He has worked as a colorist, letterer, inker, penciller, and art director in digital and print comics, posters, brochures, trading cards, magazines and scores of projects for Marvel Comics, DC Comics, Dark Horse, Random House, Papercutz, and many others. His recent projects include the Independent Publisher Book Award-winning God Woke written by the legendary Stan Lee. Wilson is also a popular sketch card artist who has work for Topps, Upper Deck, Cryptozoic Entertainment, and Dynamite Entertainment. In his spare time, Wilson works on his creator-owned comicbooks Team Kaiju and Ninja Mouse Published by Section 8 Comics.

Wilson lives in New York City, where he attended the High School of Art & Design. He received his Bachelor of Fine Arts Degree in Graphic Design from Mercy College. Wilson is super-talented, modest, and a true pro. We're very happy to have such a top talent contribute not only to THE LOUD HOUSE, but to other Papercutz graphic novels such as THE CASAGRANDES, as well.

But here's the real point of mentioning Mr. Ramos's lettering in this column—it really is "Loud and Clear." The lettering in every volume of THE LOUD HOUSE (and THE CASAGRANDES) is larger than the lettering in almost all our other Papercutz graphic novels. Traditionally in comics, larger lettering indicates that the words are louder. As for being "clear," that's something we strive for in every Papercutz graphic novel. We never want anyone to be confused, to not know which character is speaking, or to not know in which order to read the word balloons. For accomplishing all that, for making every volume of THE LOUD HOUSE loud and clear, we thank you, Mr. Ramos.

And just one more thing I want to be loud and clear about, if you love THE LOUD HOUSE graphic novels, be sure not to miss the very next one: THE LOUD HOUSE #17 "Sibling Rivalry." And don't forget THE CASAGRANDES #4—we're running a special preview of that on the very next page. We're sure you'll enjoy it!

Thanks,

Jim

STAY IN TOUCH!

EMAIL: salicrup@papercutz.com
WEB: papercutz.com
TWITTER: @papercutzgn
INSTAGRAM: @papercutzgn
FACEBOOK: PAPERCUTZGRAPHICNOVELS
FANMAIL: Papercutz, 160 Broadway, Suite 700, East Wing, New York, NY 10038

Go to papercutz.com and sign up for the free Papercutz e-newsletter!

"MEOW OR NEVER"

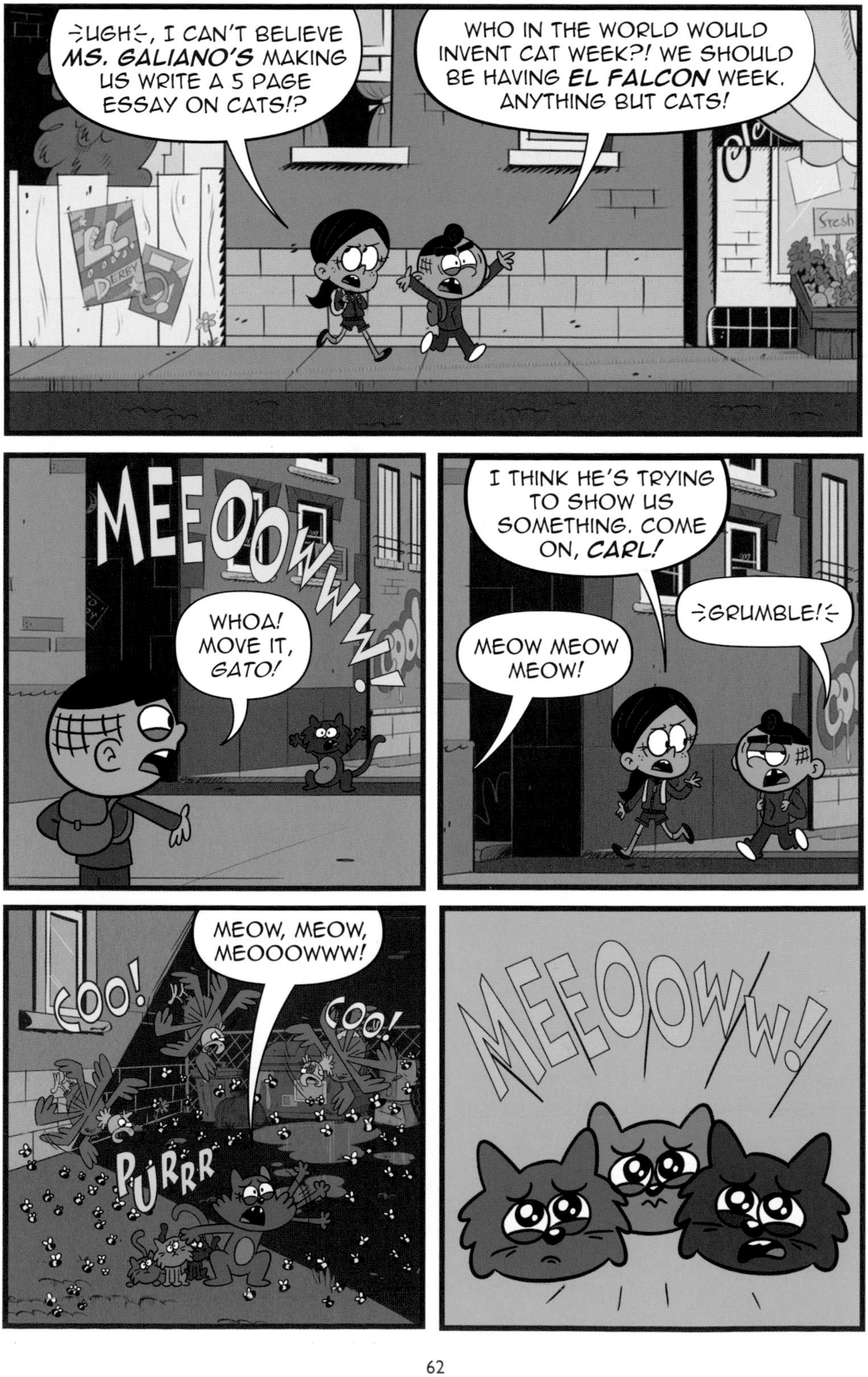
UGH, I CAN'T BELIEVE MS. GALIANO'S MAKING US WRITE A 5 PAGE ESSAY ON CATS!?
WHO IN THE WORLD WOULD INVENT CAT WEEK?! WE SHOULD BE HAVING EL FALCON WEEK. ANYTHING BUT CATS!
MEEOOWWW!
WHOA! MOVE IT, GATO!
I THINK HE'S TRYING TO SHOW US SOMETHING. COME ON, CARL!
GRUMBLE!
MEOW MEOW MEOW!
MEOW, MEOW, MEOOOWWW!
COO!
COO!
PURRR
MEEOOWW!

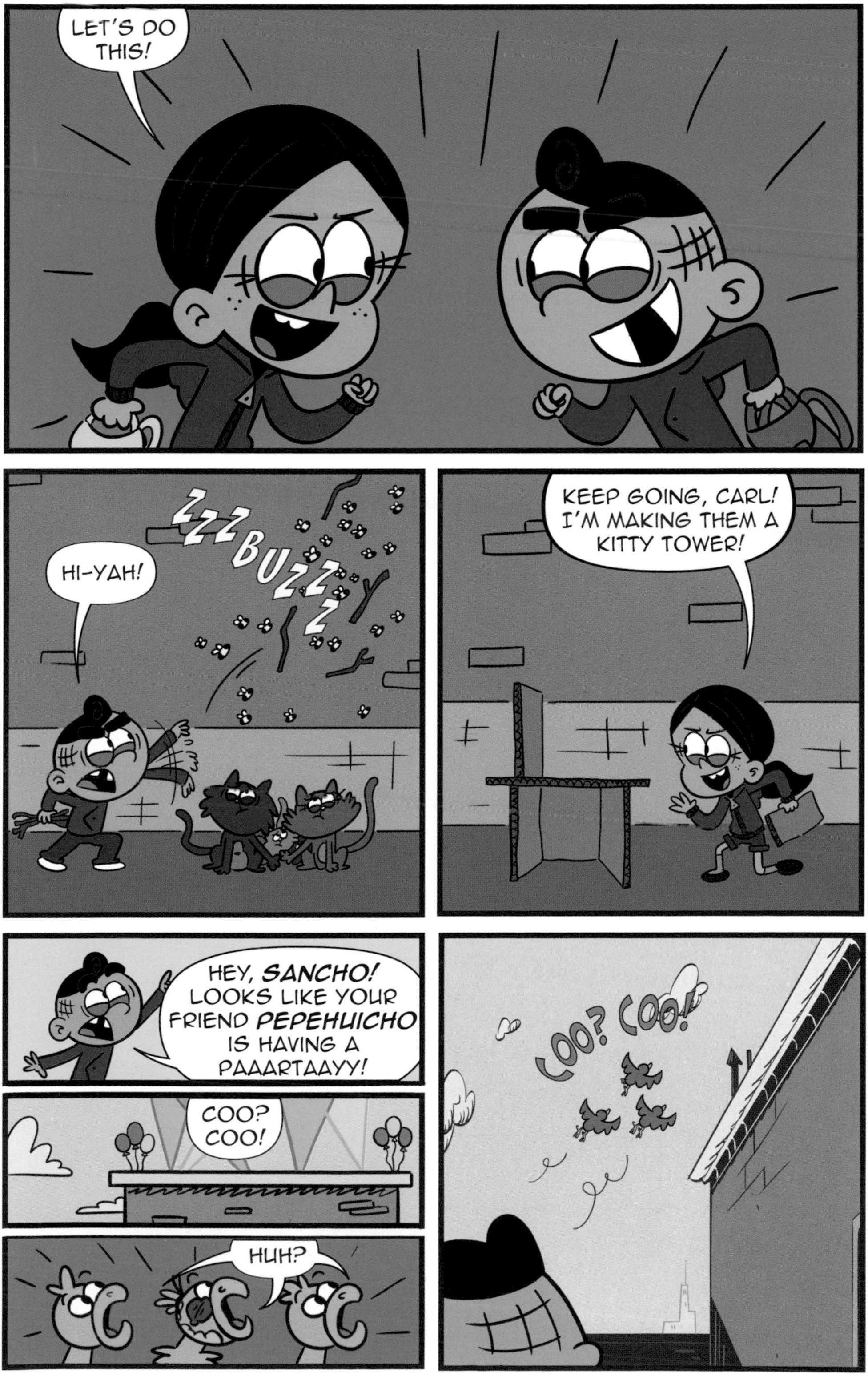
LET'S DO THIS!
HI-YAH!
ZZZBUZZZZ
KEEP GOING, CARL! I'M MAKING THEM A KITTY TOWER!
HEY, SANCHO! LOOKS LIKE YOUR FRIEND PEPEHUICHO IS HAVING A PAAARTAAYY!
COO? COO!
HUH?
COO? COO!

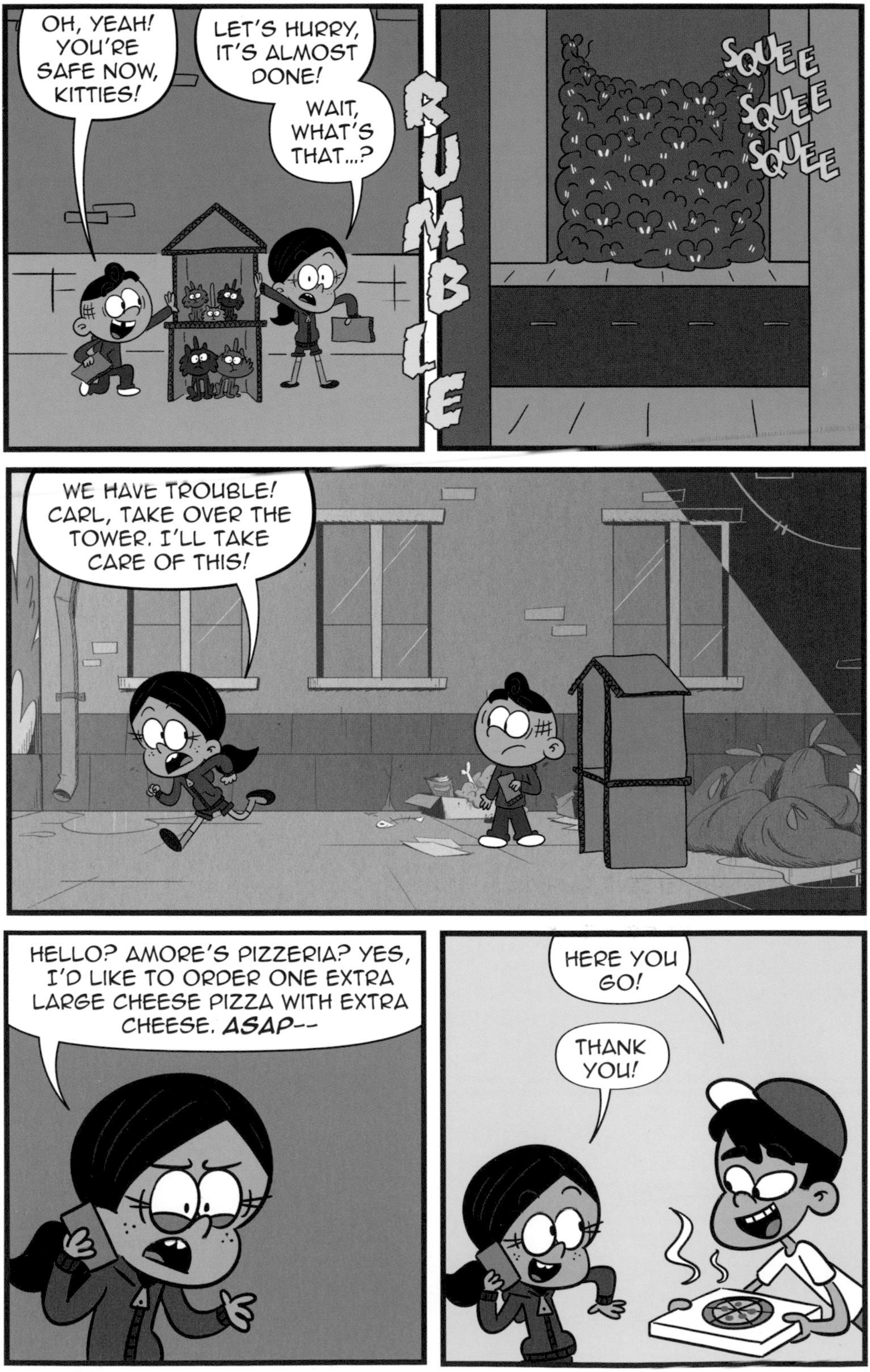
OH, YEAH! YOU'RE SAFE NOW, KITTIES!
LET'S HURRY, IT'S ALMOST DONE!
WAIT, WHAT'S THAT...?
RUMBLE
SQUEEE
SQUEEE
SQUEEE
WE HAVE TROUBLE! CARL, TAKE OVER THE TOWER. I'LL TAKE CARE OF THIS!
HELLO? AMORE'S PIZZERIA? YES, I'D LIKE TO ORDER ONE EXTRA LARGE CHEESE PIZZA WITH EXTRA CHEESE. ASAP--
HERE YOU GO!
THANK YOU!

Don't miss THE CASAGRANDES #4 coming soon to your favorite bookseller and library!